To

Kevin & Janel Jackson
Your God-made Marriage
is forever blessed.

From

[signature]

Date

GOD-MADE MARRIAGE

Enjoying Marital Bliss as the Creator Intends

Henry and Lara Emmanuel

God-Made Marriage

Book Layout Design and Printing by
Cornerstone Publishing
www.cornerstonepublishers.com

Author's Contact

For speaking engagement or to order books by Henry & Lara Emmanuel

121 Grandview Avenue
Staten Island, New York 10303
www.godmademarriage.com
Phone: 844-4-GOD-MADE
Email: godmademarriage@gmail.com

Copy Editor: Mark Steven Long
Cover Design - Toscom Creativity

Printed in the United States of America

DEDICATION

To all the God-Made Marriages.

May God's love continually guide and keep you.

Contents

Introduction

Lara

I remember the day Henry proposed to me like it was yesterday. He got down on one knee and asked, "Will you marry me?"

I immediately remembered my mother, who had been through several failed relationships prior to marrying my father. I remembered my sister, who had also been in several failed relationships with men who made empty marriage promises, some of whom she had children with. She passed away right before her thirtieth birthday, unmarried, still searching for a true love that she never found. I remembered how many times her heart had been broken by men, and how she had made me promise never to take a man merely for his words, but to know for sure that he was genuine.

So I said no the first two times Henry had proposed to me, and I told him to be patient until I knew for sure. Rather than the yes he was expecting to hear the third time, I answered his question with the question "Why?" He seemed baffled, but I needed to know why he wanted to marry me. I knew I wanted to get married just once in my lifetime and grow old with my husband. I did not want the history of failed relationships and marriages in my family to be repeated in my life. I needed to know why he would want to spend the rest of his life with me. He answered all my questions truthfully and convinced me that God had made me especially for him. I looked deeply into his eyes almost like I could see into his soul and knew he was genuine, so I said, "Yes, I will marry you."

Henry

When Lara and I got married on New Year's Day, 1994, I had no prior experience with marriage or living with a woman other than my mother and sisters. The only thing I knew about marriage was what I saw my parents display at home. My father was a very hard-working, family-oriented man whose wife catered to almost all his needs. Therefore, I expected Lara to be just like my mom, even though I was nothing close to what my father was at the time.

Our marriage ran into a road block just a few hours into the marriage, and I ended up asking myself, "What have you done to yourself, Henry?" The first year of our marriage was the worst year of our relationship. My expectations of a wife had not been met, and at this point I was convinced that it was a big mistake, that I had picked a woman who was nothing like my mother.

Who would save me from this error? I was crying

inside, even as I looked macho on the outside. Boy, did she give me a run for my money. Our first year anniversary was nothing but stormy. After the finger-pointing and the blame game, we both agreed to resolve our situation, not by going out and celebrating but by sitting down and working things out.

It was important that we find the root of our problems and work them out, since we were both still in love with each other. I came up with the idea for us to write down everything we thought we were doing or not doing that made us unhappy. That was mistake number two on my part. She ended up writing two full pages, while I had only one thing written down.

Some of her complaints were hard to swallow but they were true, and I quickly realized that while I wanted a woman like my mother, I had never taken the time to be the kind of man my father was. You see, the kind of man my father was helped shaped the kind of woman my mother became. My father was serving his wife and family while I was demanding to be served. I quickly realized the missing ingredient in our marriage, the emotional disconnection my wife was feeling, and why my expectations were not met.

Ladies and gentlemen, one of the secrets of a great marriage is serving each other. This revelation gave birth to a whole new me, and I have since made a conscious decision to spend time investing in my marriage through serving. I have not perfected it yet, but I have made great strides and seen great results in my marriage.

God-Made Marriage

We will be sharing the God-given wisdom we have gained in this book. We know you, too, can make great strides and see great results in your marriage as you read this book and put this wisdom into practice.

Whether you just want to read a good book on marriage, become more aware of your individual and spousal needs, steer clear of pitfalls, learn how to effectively communicate or improve your problemsolving skills, which you need to build a strong, satisfying and enduring marriage, this book has something for every couple.

Marriage is work—but it is not hard work, it is "heart work." Our goal is to put your heart to work, to advance your marriage or repair the damage done to your relationship over the years, by helping you realize God has placed you together for a purpose. We also hope to provide opportunities to discover how to enrich and empower your marriage with God at its center.

With God's Word, our experiences from different stages of our marriage of twenty-five years, as well as other personal examples, this book will help you take your marriage to the next level.

CHAPTER ONE

God-Made Marriage Versus Man-Made Marriage

I praise you because of the wonderful way you created me. Everything you do is marvelous! Of this I have no doubt.
—Psalm 139:14 (CEV)

Marriage is good. We know some readers may find it hard to believe, but God, the Creator of marriage, calls it a good thing. No matter how much you try to work on your marriage outside of God, it won't work as good as it would with God in it. Marriage is one of God's greatest ways of demonstrating His love and an expression of Christ's love for the church. Although marriage has been trivialized it is a serious thing and should never be entered into lightly. Although times have changed, and society has evolved, the godly principles of marriage have not changed. It is a universal principle and the building block of civilization. Marriage is the key to stability, progress, peace, and joy in any society. It is the safest relationship on earth and the oldest institution on the planet; it has been around since the beginning of time. Most people enter into a marriage with the dream of living happily ever after, yet so many of these happily-ever-after dreams end in nightmares when couples fail to use God's principles for marriage.

One major challenge today is having a happy and fruitful marriage. Society appears to be focused on economic prosperity, and many are engrossed in their careers to the detriment of marital life. It is possible to have a career and a healthy marriage of love, understanding, joy, and peace. We believe that if couples are armed with the right information from the Creator of marriage—God—and with a mutual commitment to success, even the unhealthiest relationships will experience healing, and maturity will be developed. Unfortunately, our society does not require that men and women go through some form of training before saying, "I do." However, it is important that couples go through some form of training to help guide them into this beautiful union. For this reason, we always recommend pre-marital classes before couples get married and post-marital sessions as needed.

Every man and woman want to marry the perfect person or as some would say "my dream spouse" or "soul mate." Unfortunately, there is no such thing as the perfect woman or man. No one ever get to marry their dream man or woman, except in Hollywood—and we all know how that usually ends. For years the model for marriage across the globe has been to look for Mr. or Mrs. Right, fall in love, and get married, and if you run into problems you just fall out of love, get a divorce, and start the process all over again with another partner.

It is sad to know that divorce has been glamorized to the point that many now have divorce parties. Many divorcées (we're not including those who were in abusive marriages) convince themselves that the decision is in the best interests of everyone in the family and fall for the delusion that the grass is greener on the other side. They then go in pursuit of the next Mr. or Mrs. Right.

> *A God-made marriage is not as much about finding someone perfect and totally compatible as it is about two imperfect people deciding to commit to each other despite their imperfections and differences.*

In a God-made marriage, the prerequisite for marriage is that you first be right before searching for Mr. or Mrs. Right. Quite often we hear couples blame God for their failed marriages, but a closer look often reveals that God was never a part of it. Even if He was a part of it at the beginning, it is important that you keep Him in the marriage for the duration. The moment you take God out of the equation, your marriage is headed for disaster. Just as we consult with the manufacturer's manual to know how to properly use a product, so also we need to consult with God, the Creator of marriage. God-made marriage starts with God and is intended to end when death separates husband and wife.

Anything that is God-made is carefully thought of and created by God with precise purpose and a dependable outcome. It has God's stamp of approval, and it is sustained by Him. It is pure, safe, and 100 percent guaranteed to work as intended by God.

On the other hand, whatever is man-made is created or manufactured by human beings. It is therefore not guaranteed to work as intended. It is subject to change and recalls from time to time due to malfunctions. We are sure you must have had a product that was recalled at some point.

There are no recalls on anything God-made, because they are made perfectly by a perfect God. A God-made marriage is not as much about finding someone perfect and totally compatible as it is about two imperfect people deciding to commit to each other despite their imperfections and differences, and following the guidelines for marriage from a perfect God.

God-made marriage reflects God's perfect love, and Christ's relationship with the church is likened to a marriage. You cannot take God out of marriage, because marriage was His idea. It is difficult to manage what you did not create. Just as a car cannot run without an engine, a marriage cannot work well without God and His principles. He is the only One able to help you manage your life and your marriage effectively. The very first marriage ever recorded was between Adam and Eve. After God created Adam, He put him in the garden to work and to take care of it. God later noticed that although Adam was in a beautiful environment surrounded by beautiful animals, none of them was suitable to provide the companionship that Adam needed. God said, "It is not good for man to be alone." God therefore made a suitable helper in the person of Eve and presented her to Adam. God blessed them and told them to "Prosper! Reproduce! Fill Earth! Take charge!" (Gen. 1:28 MSG). She was clearly the best gift ever based on Adam's reaction when he first set his eyes on her.

"This is it!" Adam exclaimed. "She is part of my own bone and flesh! Her name is 'woman' because she was taken out of a man." —Genesis 2:23 (TLB)

Henry

What God intends is for every man to find his "this is it" woman to share his life with forever. There are about four billion females on earth and it is interesting to know that one stands out as the "this is it" for every man. The Bible says, "He who finds a wife find a good thing and obtains favor from God." I cannot describe the joy I had in my heart when I found my "this is it" Lara. The day she agreed to marry me, I was ecstatic, and I really do not know how I drove from Coney Island to Staten Island that night. The most beautiful girl in the world had just agreed to share her life with me forever. I made it known to anyone who cared to listen that I was no longer searching for the right woman, because I had found her. Folks around me saw changes in me. I was told that I smiled a lot more. I went everywhere I could with Lara. It was surely one of the defining moments of my life. I suddenly realized I was never going to be alone ever again, and it was just a great feeling. I am sure you also can remember the day you found your "this is it" wife.

There are fundamental differences between a God-made marriage and a man-made marriage. A God-made marriage is the relationship designed by God for every married couple to share unending love, passion, joy, and peace. This marriage is very different from a man-made one.

Now let us look at some of the differences between a God-made marriage and a man-made marriage.

MAN-MADE MARRIAGE

In a man-made marriage, the relationship is adulterated because it has been weakened or lessened in purity by the removal of God and the addition of elements suitable to mankind. This marriage is unreal and unnatural in so many ways. It inaccurately depicts the purpose of marriage and it is very often overshadowed by unrealistic expectations with insincere motives. Love is conditional in this marriage, and man's emotion always gets in the way. It is a "me, myself, and I alone" marriage.

It is a contract, not a covenant. Couples treat this kind of marriage like a test tube experiment in which they must keep performing with different specimens until they get it right. They come up their own idea of what marriage should be and hope it will work. Both spouses tend to put only 50 percent effort in the marriage. They are mostly there to help themselves to whatever they can get out of the marriage, rather than what they can add to it.

Prenuptial and postnuptial agreement is often required in this marriage. Both spouses mostly consider each other dispensable. So if it is not working they just move on to the next person. "In sickness and in health, for better or for worse, for richer or for poorer, and till death do us part" is often taken out of the marriage vows and replaced with whatever is convenient for them. They'll often say things like "It is my way or the highway." "If it is not working I get out of it." "If it breaks I throw it away and get another one." "We will stay married for as long as we can stand each other." "We will stay married until one of us is broke or falls sick." "If I am not happy it ain't happening." When circumstances change, they give up. We live in a fallen world; therefore, the world's view on marriage is a faulty system that can result to irreconcilable differences and ultimately broken homes.

We cannot entrust our homes to this kind of marriage. Man-made marriage continues to evolve from one generation to another, with each generation redefining marriage based on what suits them. Just because something has a stamp of approval from mankind and is favored by the majority does not necessarily mean it has God's approval.

In the last twenty years the divorce rate among baby boomers has increased by 50 percent, and as a result Generation X and the millennials have shifted from the traditional sense of marriage with longevity to a temporal marriage of convenience. This marriage falls apart when the storms of life, such as unemployment, bills, bankruptcies, sickness, substance abuse, addictions, pride, and overbearing in-laws, show up. God never intended for marriages to fail. His plan is for marriages to last until death. Marriage is God's idea, and divorce is man's idea. Since marriage is God's idea, He alone has the power and tools to keep it. Only His principles will work, and it is a universal principle. God says He hates divorce, not the people getting the divorce. Why? Because divorce is devastating for everyone involved, especially the children and the consequences often last a lifetime. God hates to see what divorce does to lives and families which is the opposite of what He wants for every family.

"Their worship is a farce, for they teach man-made ideas as commands from God. For you ignore God's law and substitute your own tradition." Then he said, "You skillfully sidestep God's law in order to hold on to your own tradition."
—Mark 7:7-9 (NLT)

GOD-MADE MARRIAGE

A God-made marriage is a covenant, not a contract. Contracts are legally binding, but covenants are spiritually binding. This covenant relationship is between a man and a woman who agree to live and function together under God's revealed principles until death do them part. It is a divinely established lifestyle that demonstrates unconditional love. God, the Creator of marriage, intended for marriage to last a lifetime and its legacy passed from one generation to another.

A God-made marriage is an experience, not an experiment. You experience love, joy, peace, harmony, favor, and so much more together. You experience life together in stages. From the experience of two lives becoming one, to starting a family, to handling challenges, to growing old together and passing the baton to your children. This marriage is a marriage of longevity filled with a lifetime of experience and cherished memories. Unlike a man-made marriage, where couples keep experimenting with several partners, the formula for a successful marriage has already been established by God Himself. A man leaves his father and his mother, cleaves to his wife, becomes one flesh with her, and follows God's manual.

> *A God-made marriage is an experience, not an experiment. You experience love, joy, peace, harmony, favor, and so much more together.*

PLEASING GOD IN YOUR MARRIAGE

So we make it our goal to please Him. —2 Corinthians 5:9 (NIV)

Lara

Henry and I struggled on many fronts in the early years of our marriage. It took commitment and the proper application of God's principle for our marriage to overcome those challenges, and we are now able share this wisdom with you. We were at a conference many years ago, and while introducing his wife the guest preacher said that she had never given him any problem. I turned to Henry and said, "Well, that is one claim you will never be able to make in this lifetime." In the early years of our marriage, I never backed down from arguments. Winning arguments were like trophies for me. Some of my favorites lines back then were "Don't start what you can't finish" and "You are not going to win this argument." As he often does during one of these arguments, Henry gave in and apologized for peace's sake, even though I knew he was not wrong and I realized my actions were not right. I was merely taking advantage of a good husband who walks away from arguments for the sake of peace in our home. In a God-made marriage it is not a matter of winning or losing, it is all about doing what is right and what pleases God.

It does not please God that you treat others so well but you treat your spouse so badly. It does not please God that you respect others but disrespect your spouse. It does not please God that your coworkers see you at your best, but your spouse and children see you at your worst. It does not please God that you speak softly to others but yell at your spouse and children. It does not please God that you gladly bring lunch for your supervisor and coworkers but you are reluctant to cook dinner at home. It does not please God that you are so patient with others but very impatient with your spouse and children. It does not please God that you volunteer to help others but refuse to help your spouse at home. It does not please God that you can spend countless hours hanging out with your friends and no time with your family. It does not please God that you meet your work's deadline but still have not fixed the leaky sink after six months. It does not please God that you clean up after yourself on your job but won't do the same at home. It does not please God that you have external success outside but are considered an internal failure at home. Any kind of abuse—physical, verbal, emotional—does not please God. Your spouse and children deserve the best of you, not the worst of you. The result of your commitment to please God in your marriage will be a pleased spouse.

Motivations are the real reason behind our decisions and actions in life. If you therefore make pleasing God the motivating factor in your marriage, it becomes the driving force of decision-making that honors God. It allows you to evaluate every decision by asking yourself this question: "Will this action of mine please God?" Pleasing God should be your goal in your marriage, because when you please God you will gladly please your spouse. This comes before sexual expression and fulfillment, happiness, the bearing of children, and provision. The challenge, of course, is that it is totally selfless living. The pursuit of happiness in marriage should be led by an undeniable, relentless effort to please God. In the marriage covenant we have no other choice as to how we live; we owe it to God to live for Him, to make Him our first priority and final authority. To accomplish this, you will have to give up your selfish daily desires and stop making decisions based on what is best for you alone rather than what is best for your marriage.

GUIDELINES FOR THE GOD-MADE MARRIAGE EXERCISES

The exercises in this book are designed to help you better understand yourselves, and you should not use them to point fingers at each other. Find a quiet place and give each other your undivided attention. Do not do these exercises without first reading each chapter. Taking turns to ask and answer these questions will not only help you understand each other better, it will also help you become better listeners. Make eye contact, hold each other, and do not interrupt or judge each other. Listen wholeheartedly, and be open minded and willing to learn. Answer each question honestly and calmly.

Exercise: Take turns to ask each other the following questions

1. In what areas is our marriage reflective of a God-made marriage?
2. Where do you see our marriage five years from now?
3. What should be our top three priorities this year?

Two Becoming One

For this cause a man shall leave his father and his mother,
and shall cleave to his wife; and they shall become one flesh.
—Genesis 2:24 (NASB77)

THE PROCESS

God is very precise in all His ways including marriage, and He precisely emphasized the importance of the two becoming one. This, however, cannot be done until the man leaves his father and his mother. The two becoming one is a process; it does not happen overnight. It takes time to become the good husband and wife you desire. We will go into more details when we get to the stages of marriage. God-made marriage requires oneness and the proof of love lies in the willingness to become one with your spouse.

"A man shall leave his father and mother . . ."

Notice that it is the man who is told to leave his father and mother so he can cleave to his wife. God knows that the man needs his wife, and to fully bond with her he must leave the only other relationship in which he has felt safe all his life—the one with his parents. Leaving his father and mother's house allows him to develop and have a clean canvas to create new memories.

> **God-made marriage requires oneness and the proof of love lies in the willingness to become one with your spouse.**

Both spouses must have functional independence emotionally and financially from their parents. Leaving his parents facilitates his cleaving to his wife. Very often, you see spouses still totally dependent on their parents emotionally even after they have physically left. Leaving is therefore more emotional than physical, and it is a continuous process, not a one-time event.

"And shall cleave to his wife . . ." means the man becomes intimately acquainted with his wife so they can build a stronger bond. This is how the unity of the husband and wife is formed. You are stronger together, you work better together, and you shine brighter together when you cleave. You become totally committed and loyal to each other. There is no loss of respect to parents, but a shift in loyalty toward the spouse. For the purpose of becoming one, the man must leave his parents and cleave unto his wife. Here we see a switch in loyalty while still relating to his parents with respect. Most parents, especially mothers, have a major problem with the shift in loyalty and often resent their son or daughter-in-law for this reason. You cannot cleave until you leave. Cleaving entails spending time in getting to know and cling to your spouse. This cannot be achieved without leaving your family of origin.

"And they shall become one flesh" means that you are inseparable. It also means no one dominates the relationship, because you are a team and you do everything together as a team. What God has joined together let no one put asunder. Part of God's goal in marriage is to unite the husband and his wife as one. One direction, one purpose, one vision, one language. You don't necessarily have to like the same things to become one, but you must learn to agree even when you don't like the same things. Make decisions that are best for your marriage even if it's not what you wanted. Becoming one flesh also refers to sexual union and intimacy. I believe we can learn how to become one when we look at how we became one with God.

The scripture says God loves us, and to prove it He gave us His best—Jesus Christ, who died for us to secure for us an everlasting life with God. To ensure that we are in fellowship with Him, He puts His Spirit in us for strength, guidance, and better relationship with the Father. For companionship the Holy Spirit is there for the believer. Likewise, husband and wife must be each other's companion, in constant fellowship and unified in the bond of peace. You will therefore become fruitful in your walk and commitment to each other and to God.

God-Made Marriage

Marriage can and should work the very first time if entered rightly. If it did not work out well for you previously, then with proper understanding and guidance you should succeed in your next marriage. Spouses are required to do everything to make it work and have the attitude. There are no shortcuts; whatever you put into it is what you will get out of it. Imagine two lives joined together as one, then begin a new cycle of life by starting their own family and raising their own children. The couple has become one: one life, one family, one purpose, one mission. No more "me, myself, and I." No more "my plans, my career, my ways, my goals, my happiness"; it is now "our lives together."

It saddens us when we hear people say they ended their marriage because they were no longer happy. We understand the concept of "happily ever after," but it is an unrealistic expectation. You will not be happy 24/7. Happiness is a choice, and you are primarily responsible for your own happiness. Happily married couples are two individuals who became one but have individually decided to be happy despite whatever life deals them at different stages of their marriage. You must therefore place great value on your marriage by investing yourself in it.

You can win and experience a winning atmosphere in your marriage if you will commit to the Word of God and make it your first priority and your final authority. If couples do not learn and understand God's plan for marriage, they will end up with a worldview of marriage that often results in divorce. We believe that a God-centered marriage results in a changed lifestyle and a perpetual growth. This kind of change and growth, if genuinely undertaken, will ultimately help you overcome any challenge that shows up in your marriage. Understanding marriage—knowing why you are married and why you should stay married—is vital for the longevity of your marriage. For this reason, couples must be headed in the same direction and have the same purpose in marriage.

Can two people walk together without agreeing on the direction? —Amos 3:3 (NLT)

The purpose of marriage must be elevated above your reasons for getting married. Couples often say they got married because they make each other happy, they are soul mates, they bring out the best in each other, and so on. But when the one who once made you happy now makes you sad, when your soul mate now acts like a hell mate, when the one who used to bring out the best in you now brings out the worst in you, the purpose of marriage will sustain you. Please note that the strength of your marriage will be tested. Your feelings will be hurt from time to time. But if you make purpose the strength of your marriage, then on any day you don't feel like you once used to feel about your spouse, purpose becomes the strength that holds your marriage up. In other words, the integrity structure of your marriage will not be compromised when problem arise.

Your approach toward marriage should be a God-centered view that brings honor to God and reminds you He alone is the source and the sustainer of your marriage. As a result, you will learn to overcome natural challenges with spiritual understanding. We live in a fallen world and the world's view on marriage is faulty; therefore, you cannot entrust yours to it. From one generation to another the world keeps redefining what marriage and family is, but God's definition of marriage stays the same.

You cannot live outside the structure you have created for your marriage. Whatever state you are right now in your marriage relationship is as a result of what you have allowed, either good or bad. The good news is your marriage can change for the better when you and your spouse make the commitment to allow the Word of God to be your first priority and your final authority.

Lara

When Henry ("Mr. Save Money") and I ("Mrs. Shopaholic") got married, it was quite a challenge to come to an agreement on our finances. Henry was fine with his one suit and sport jacket, but I needed to keep up with my trendy outfits. First, he told me I needed to cut down on my shopping, and I was somewhat fine with that. But when he said we needed to combine our income and have a monthly budget, I went off. I was fine with "his money" becoming "my money," but "my money" becoming "his money"? That was a no-no. I sort of agreed to a budget after several arguments, but I would still go shopping and hide stuff in the trunk of my car, the garage, and the closets just so he wouldn't find them. Of course, he found some of my secret stashes, and we ended up arguing about them.

Then Henry did something that changed my mind and helped me to understand what he had been saying all along. He reminded me what the vision of our marriage was, and together we were able set our shortand long-term goals. Cutting down on shopping did not make me happy, but it was in the best interest of our family to set financial goals and have a budget. As a result, Henry and I were able to buy our first house, which was one of the items in our five-year plan. I became a clearance rack expert, and to this day will still go through the clearance rack first in every store. In every marriage there is a spender and a saver; therefore, you must always have a budget. Be sure to prioritize your needs over your wants. Write the vision down and make it plain (Habakkuk 2:2).

Exercise: Do this together

1. Calculate and stay within the household budget (food, rent, car payment, etc.).

2. Set savings goals and create a plan to pay off your debts: loans, credit cards, mortgage.

3. Determine your short-term and long-term goals.

CHAPTER THREE
Stronger Together

Two people are better off than one, for they can help each other succeed. If one person falls, the other can reach out and help. But someone who falls alone is in real trouble. Likewise, two people lying close together can keep each other warm. But how can one be warm alone? A person standing alone can be attacked and defeated, but two can stand back-to-back and conquer. Three are even better, for a triple-braided cord is not easily broken. —Ecclesiastes 4:9–12 (NLT)

Marriage is not a solo act, so do not try to be great alone, but be great together because you are stronger together. In a God-made marriage, two flawed people never give up on each other but help each other be the best that they can be.

"Two people are better off than one, for they can help each other succeed" (Eccl. 4:9).

When you work together, you succeed together by helping each other do things you can't do individually. You will get more done faster and better together than you would by yourselves. Help each other succeed and never be intimidated by each other's success.

"If one falls down, his friend can help him up, but pity the man who falls and has no one to help him up!" (Eccl. 4:10). No marriage is free from trouble so help each other during difficult times. Be ready to pick up the spouse who is down during those difficult moments. Never let your spouse go through tough times alone.

"Also, if two lie down together, they will keep warm. But how can one keep warm alone?" (Eccl.4:11). Provide warmth and loving comfort to each other as needed. Show care and be ready to encourage. Be sensitive to each other's needs and quick to pick each other up as needed.

"Though one may be overpowered, two can defend themselves. A cord of three strands is not quickly broken" (Eccl. 4:12). Just like a three-cord strand is not easily broken, so also is a marriage with God at the center. You can overcome whatever life throws at you thereby turning oppositions to opportunities and setbacks into comebacks.

Although you are stronger together, you are strongest with God. With God, you are a team that cannot be overcome or defeated. You are valuable to each other and your marriage adds value to you when you begin to view your spouse as a "sole mate" not just soul mate.

As Realtors, we use the terms "Valued Clients" for property owners and "Valued Customers" for tenants. The Valued Clients will invest thousands of dollars for the maintenance and upgrade of their properties. The Valued Customer will not invest thousands of dollars into the same property but would rather move out and rent another one. The reason is that the Valued Client has placed value on the property and will continue to invest in it for better usage, thereby increasing the value of the property. Likewise, if you place a great value in your marriage, you will invest in it and have a great return. The greatest mistake any spouse can make is to think that they will be better off alone without their spouse. You are better together and stronger together when you realize you are a team. It also becomes easier to make healthy changes needed in your relationship. The truth therefore is that:

- You may bring more to the table than your spouse, but you are better together and stronger together.

- You may make more sense than your spouse, but you are better together and stronger together.

- You may do more around the house than your spouse, but you are better together and stronger together.

To be stronger together, you both must be headed in the same direction and have the same purpose in marriage. You are no longer two people but one, which is God's original intent. Any misdirection will create problems that could sink you both as well as the marriage. The weight must never tilt to one side. A husband and his wife must function like the two wings on a bird.

That's why a man leaves his father and mother and gets married.

He becomes like one person with his wife. Then they are no longer two people, but one for life. —Mark 10:7-8 (CEV)

This scripture is talking about you both going in the same direction and having the same purpose. You must work together or the marriage will never get off the ground, even if you have been married a long time. You can stay successfully married only when the purpose for marriage is stronger and louder than the challenges you are going through.

MARRIED LIFE MANAGEMENT

A God-made marriage requires good management to function effectively. Managing your marriage involves timing, planning, prioritizing, effective communication, and problem solving. Manage your life very well by making time for each other and the things that matter the most. Learn to prioritize and make the most of your time together. You cannot manage your life if you do not manage your time well. You cannot manage your married life if you do not manage your emotions. If you choose to do what is right, then your emotions will catch up. Stop wanting the marriage that others have; manage your own marriage well, and it will be as good as the others or even better. There are three things you cannot recover: the word after it is spoken, the moment after it is missed, and the time after it is gone. You should therefore be very careful to avoid misusing these things.

The word after it is spoken—Words are powerful. Words can make or break. Be careful not to hurt or break each other's heart with your words. It is better not to speak when you are angry than to speak and regret what you said. I am sure we have all said something to someone we wish we could take back. I know it is common for people to try and take back what they have said. The truth of the matter is that we cannot take back our words after they are spoken, and regardless of how many times we say we are sorry, those words will still hurt. Therefore, be slow to speak, watch your mouth, and guide what comes out of it.

The moment after it is missed—Moment creates momentum, so build on the momentum of every moment, and be ready to cease each moment to build precious memories that would last a lifetime. Don't just collect things, collect moments also. It is not the big things that are important in a marriage but the little moments of laughter and joy. Cherish those moments and cherish the life you have. If you are going to be there, then be there. Do not let your body be in one location while your mind is somewhere else. It saddens us when we see families that could be enjoying their time at a restaurant or at home having dinner together all glued to their smartphones instead of engaging in conversation. Pay attention to every moment, because you won't know which moments will count unless you pay attention.

The time after it is gone—Time is a precious gift given to us by God and should never be wasted or taken for granted. Do not let the busyness of life rob you of quality time together. Do you remember when you fell in love? You made time for each other despite your busy schedules. Those times together made you fall in love, so do not stop doing the things that you both enjoy together. Whether it's going for a walk, sharing a dessert, talking and reminiscing about the past, laughing together, or playing together. Make sure you give each other your undivided attention every day. The quality time you spend together is a great deposit into your marriage account that will yield dividends in the future. Your best life together is now, so make each day count. Have a great day on purpose.

Exercise: Take turns to ask each other the following questions

1. In what ways do I act like I am still single rather than married to you?

2. Please forgive me for the times I left you out and made decisions alone.

3. What can I do to ensure that we stay stronger together?

CHAPTER FOUR

The Unstoppable Power of Love

Always keep me in your heart and wear this bracelet to remember me by. The passion of love bursting into flame is more powerful than death, stronger than the grave. —Song of Solomon 8:6 (CEV)

Love is not a feeling; it is different from the feelings that accompany love. Love is powerful, and it is unstoppable. Love is a choice, so always choose love. Love is sacrificial. Love is active. It is an action, not an attitude. Love is giving, and it is selfless. Love is true and does not say yes when it means no. Love requires total honesty and transparency. Love will cut through any obstacle or barrier to fulfill its purpose. The foundation of a God-made marriage is unconditional love.

What's love got to do with it? Everything!!! You go from falling in love to being in love to walking in love. Love is simply the giving of oneself to another. You will become unstoppable when your marriage covenant is solid. The foundation of every lasting marriage is love.

The word "love" is probably the most misused word in the world. It is used to express feelings not only toward others but also toward animals, food, places, and things. Feeling is often misconstrued as love; if a spouse feels a certain way and is not in agreement with the other spouse, the other spouse tends to feel unloved. There is absolutely no doubt that emotions accompany love, but it is a very minute part of love. Feelings or emotions will change depending on what is happening around you, but love will never change.

We recently came across a video circulating on social media where a woman said, and we quote, "Love is not a good reason to get married, because marriage is not a vehicle of love as much as it is a vehicle for building foundations, wealth, legacy, and intimacy." Although marriage is a vehicle for building, it still takes love to initiate and commit to the building. Just as a building cannot stand without a proper foundation, no marriage can stand or last without the foundation of love.

Love never gives up.

Love cares more for others than for self.

Love doesn't want what it doesn't have.

Love doesn't strut,

Doesn't have a swelled head,

Doesn't force itself on others,

Isn't always "me first,"

Doesn't fly off the handle,

Doesn't keep score of the sins of others,

Doesn't revel when others grovel,

Takes pleasure in the flowering of truth,

Puts up with anything,

Trusts God always,

Always looks for the best,

Never looks back,

But keeps going to the end.

—1 Corinthians 13:4–7 (MSG)

Everything in the above scripture is based on choices. Love chooses never to give up. Love chooses not to fly off the handle. Love chooses not to keep score of wrongdoings and so on. Love itself is therefore a choice, and you will make series of choices in the span of your marriage. Please choose rightly. The kind of love that will sustain a marriage and create a deep, intimate union between a man and a woman is God's kind of love. We must learn to love like Christ loved the Church, sacrificially.

God-made marriage is associated with God's kind of love. This is the only kind of love that sustains and strengthens a marriage. It is known as "agape love," which is an unconditional love. Agape love is sacrificial, and it is purposeful. This love is wrapped up in commitment that says to the person being loved, "Though we may disagree, I will never leave nor forsake you." It allows married couples to connect with each other emotionally, and it is deeply rooted in commitment. Inasmuch as you both need to be emotionally healthy, focus also on being committed to each other, because where your emotions may fail commitment will stand firm. Love never fails. Commitment and love go hand in hand; therefore, you cannot have one without the other. It is impossible to love your spouse and not be committed to your spouse.

Please understand that every marriage goes through periods of testing and challenges. When your marriage and your love for each other is tested, all the feelings in the world will not be able to sustain that marriage. It will take your love for God, your love for your spouse, and your commitment to each other to overcome the periods of testing.

Love is not selfish, so there is no room for selfishness in a God-made marriage. Marriage is actually a great tool to kill selfishness. We know we live in the "selfie" era, but the decisions you make as a married person can no longer be made based on self, because other lives will be affected by your selfish decisions. Therefore, your unrealistic expectations must be dealt with and reality must kick in. We recommend that you make your family picture the screen saver on all of your devices as a constant reminder that it is no longer about you. No room for slothfulness; marriage is work. It requires work to make it work. No room for childishness, because lives are at stake. Marriage is for matured people with realistic expectations. The apostle Paul said it well in 1 Corinthians 13:11 (ESV):

When I was a child, I spoke like a child, I thought like a child, I reasoned like a child. When I became a man, I gave up childish ways.

You have to detach yourself from anything or anyone that will hinder your ability to be matured and fully commit to your spouse. In a God-made marriage, God must be the first priority and the final authority in every facet of the marriage. There were times we could have allowed our emotions to get the best of us, but this phrase kept us in check and it works every time.

The most effective tool in a God-made marriage is your relationship with God. The more you love God, the more you love your spouse. The more time you spend with God, the more time you will want to spend with your spouse. The more you do for God, the more you will do for your spouse. The more you commit to God, the more you will commit to your spouse. The more you honor God, the more you will honor your spouse, and so on. Your marriage will stay strong if you submit yourselves to God and you both agree to operate under the designated structure of authority that is revealed in the Word of God.

It's troubling to see two people who once said they loved each other turn around and say they hate each other. We believe if they had the proper understanding or knowledge of love and marriage before entering into it, this sad event would have been avoided. One of the weapons the enemy (Satan) uses in marriage is lack of knowledge.

My people perish for lack of knowledge. —Hosea 4:6

The lack of godly principles and knowledge in the marriage relationship has destroyed more marriages that could have turned out great. We have been graced by God for victory in this world. You can experience victory and joy in your marriage if you apply God's principle of walking in love. God never told us to fall in love; He said to walk in love. You can fall out of love just as quickly as you fall in love. This is why so many fell in love one day and fell out of love the next day. Walking in love is a daily decision for a long-term goal. Marriage is much more than falling in love; it is also walking and staying in love. Love has been so devalued in our society and lost its true meaning. Falling in love is easy. But walking and staying in love is the real deal. Walking in love requires a tremendous amount of sacrifice, and true love is measured by the sacrifices you make.

> *Your marriage will stay strong if you submit yourselves to God and you both agree to operate under the designated structure of authority that is revealed in the Word of God.*

Therefore, be imitators of God as dear children. And walk in love, as Christ also has loved us and given Himself for us, an offering and a sacrifice to God for a sweet-smelling aroma. —Ephesians 5:1–2 (NKJV)

The proof of God's love was measured by the quality of His gift to mankind, and the proof of Jesus' love was also measured by His sacrificing His life for all. He literally loved us to death. Love goes all the way. Are you willing to go the distance for your marriage? Are you willing to pay the price of patience and inconvenience? Imagine the price Jacob paid for the love of his life, Rachel. Fourteen years of hard labor. Most men would have said, "Babe, I love you, but no woman is worth this much sacrifice so I'm out." The kind of love that sustains marriages says, "I am here for you, no matter what."

> *Most wives have no problem following and submitting to a leader; they have a problem submitting to a dictator who wants things done his way.*

Watch what God does, and then you do it, like children who learn proper behavior from their parents. Mostly what God does is love you. Keep company with him and learn a life of love. Observe how Christ loved us. His love was not cautious but extravagant. He didn't love in order to get something from us but to give everything of himself to us. Love like that. —Ephesians 5:1–2 (MSG)

Being subject to one another out of reverence for Christ. Wives, be subject to your own husbands, as [a service] to the Lord. For the husband is head of the wife, as Christ is head of the church, Himself being the Savior of the body. But as the church is subject to Christ, so also wives should be subject to their husbands in everything [respecting both their position as protector and their responsibility to God as head of the house]. Husbands, love your wives [seek the highest good for her and surround her with a caring, unselfish love], just as Christ also loved the church and gave Himself up for her.
—Ephesians 5:21–25 (AMP)

There is a call for the husband and the wife to submit to God and to each other in two different but unique ways that foster stability and strength in the home. The wife is called to submit to her husband as the head of the household, not in dictatorship but in leadership. There are fundamental differences between a dictator and a leader. A dictator rules by inspiring fear and asserting power and control, while a leader gently guides and encourages by example. Most wives have no problem following and submitting to a leader; they have a problem submitting to a dictator who wants things done his way.

A husband should evaluate himself to see if he is a dictator or a leader whenever problems arise in the area of submission. In her submission, a wife must be respectful to her husband, see him as one who is responsible for her and serves as a protector. Likewise, the husband is called to submit to his wife by loving her as Christ loves the Church—and as we all know, Christ's love for the church is sacrificial. He did not wait for the Church to act right or say the right things before He demonstrated such wonderful love toward her.

Marriage is work, but it is work done with your heart.

Good marriages don't just happen. Marriage is work. The work you put into your marriage determines the result you will get in your marriage. If you want your marriage to be successful, you must work on it. People put so much work in the relationship and then relax once they get married. Whatever you did to get your spouse to say "I do" must continue afterward unless it violates laws and the holy matrimony. You do not relent in your efforts; the work continues in order to sustain the marriage. Although marriage is work, it is work done with your heart.

There is a connection between the heart and marriage. The heart is the place of decision-making, and in marriage you will have to make a series of decisions. Our thinking, developing, and feeling are all done in the heart. Therefore, if your hearts are connected in doing what is right, you will get the right results. In heart work, couples focus first on self, being emotionally healthy, and working on being better spouses.

One of God's goals in marriage is to unite two people together in love as one. This marriage unity takes place in the heart, but if couples refuse to make that commitment in their heart, it can have a negative effect in their relationship. The right heart cannot be affected by the wrong attitude of your spouse. Even when he is angry at his wife, a husband does not stop being her protector and provider. Likewise, as angry as she may be with her husband, the wife must never stop being his helpmeet.

Becoming one happens when you both discover God's love, purpose, and plan for your marriage and these things take their place in your hearts. The two hearts must beat as one. Why the Heart? Because "out of the heart flow the issues of life" (Prov. 4:23). The heart is the deepest part of our being, where God speaks to, where changes occurs, and where issues of marriage are logged.

There are different heart conditions found in a marriage: A hardened heart condition, a wondering heart condition, and a right heart condition.

He said to them, "Moses, because of the hardness of your hearts, permitted you to divorce your wives, but from the beginning it was not so." —Matthew 19:8 (NKJV)

Most divorces are as the result of a hardened heart. A hardened heart is a negative heart condition in which the person rejects the components needed for a healthy marriage. A positive heart—a heart willing to make all the changes necessary for the success of the marriage—will promote healthy marital bliss.

A wandering heart in a marriage relationship is a heart that moves or travels about without any definite purpose or destination. This kind of heart tends to go off course from the main purpose of the marriage and as a result loses direction. Some of the signs of a wandering heart are thinking irrationally, and speaking incoherently or illogically. Generally, in life, when you lose focus from purpose, your heart will begin to wander. So too in a marriage: If there is a loss of focus from purpose, the marriage will struggle to sustain the intensity and intimacy required for the relationship to grow. Marriage should be viewed and entered into as heart work and not hard work. People get married for different reasons, and they have different expectations. When those expectations are not met, this often become the reason for ending the marriage.

In a God-made marriage, both spouses must have the right heart, right guidance, and commitment for the marriage to work. We have established that although marriage is work, it is not hard work. Marriage is heart work; therefore, whatever you put into it is what you will get out of it.

Hard work on the job often leads to tiredness and stress. When people are tired and stressed they tend to give up, shut down, or quit and look for another job. Likewise, if a marriage is treated as hard work, spouses will become tired and stressed by every challenge. They will want to give up, shut down, and quit. They may then look for another spouse, hoping this time it will be less work. This can become a pattern for life.

Henry

Heart Work is done with the recipe of love, gentleness, kindness, meekness, and patience. It reminds me of Lara's cooking. With joy she puts all the ingredients on the table, and one by one they make it into the pot. In a few minutes the room is filled with the aroma of her cooking, and everyone is drawn to the table. Likewise, a marriage mixed with the ingredients of love, gentleness, kindness, meekness, and patience will draw couples closer together, even when that marriage is tested.

If a couple is serious about improving the quality of their marital union, the heart definitely would be a good place to start, and it is never too late to develop the right heart in a marriage. All you need to do is allow the Word of God to be your first priority and your final authority. When you do so, God's values will ultimately become yours, because our values define our choices. The heart is a place of decision-making, and "out of it flow the issues of life" (Prov. 4:23). The right heart relative to marriage produces trust in the relationship, and that closes up all the gaps that could lead to separation.

The heart of her husband safely trusts her; So he will have no lack of gain. —Proverbs 31:11 (NKJV)

Exercise: Take turns to ask each other the following questions

1. In what ways can I better express more love to you?

2. What can I do to maintain peace and harmony in our marriage?

3. What changes do I need to make to our marriage better?

CHAPTER FIVE

Marriage—The Learning Institution

Marriage is a learning institution. It is called an institution because it is a place where you learn something new every day. It is the indispensable glue that holds the society together morally, socially, ethically, psychologically, and spiritually. It is now a known fact that children born and raised in a healthy marital home with love, nurturing, and stability grow up to be emotionally healthy, secure, and well-rounded.

The state of human society is the result of broken homes often caused by failed marriages. Yet marriage has become one of the most underrated and undervalued institutions in our society today. A recent survey shows that more than 50 percent of people in several parts of the world no longer believe in the institution of marriage due to the high rate of divorce.

God-Made Marriage

You learn something new each day, regardless of how long you have been married. There should never be a time in your marriage that you feel you cannot learn from either the good or the bad, the failures or the successes you encounter. It is a place where both the man and the woman fit neatly together, physically, spiritually and emotionally and neither is entirely comfortable without the other. You will learn and discover who you are really married to. You will learn your spouse's likes and dislikes. The discovery process in marriage is progressional. If you fail to discover and understand your spouse, the process will be difficult. Learning is not automatic—it requires effort.

Henry

You should spend time learning to know each other. This is a very important part of the growth process for a successful marriage. When Lara and I first got married I did not understand her, but I acted like I did and became even the more confused. I could not understand why this woman I love so dearly in courtship became a "thorn in my flesh" after we got married. It got to a point where we almost called it quits in the first year, until one day I got a revelation about this scripture:

Likewise, ye husbands, dwell with them according to knowledge, giving honor unto the wife, as unto the weaker vessel, and as being heirs together of the grace of life; that your prayers be not hindered. —1 Peter 3:7 (KJV)

Through God's help I quickly realized that my assumption of Lara was totally wrong, and the reason I had ended up making such a conclusion was because I had not taken time to know her in such a way that conveys honor to her.

In the learning process couples are expected to gain knowledge and get understanding of each other daily for the purpose of relating better. Do you know what pleases your spouse? What gets on their nerves? Have you come to recognize what each other's strengths are and help sharpen those skills? Do you know what your weaknesses are so that you can help each other overcome them?

In the learning part of marriage, intimate knowledge about your spouse is revealed to you in bits and pieces. As time passes, your wife's needs will change. The first year's need may have been love and affection. The second year she may need help with household chores. The fifth year she may need help with the kids, and the twentieth year she may need reassurance that she is still beautiful. In the learning institution of marriage, your spouse will sometimes unintentionally reveal to you that part of them you never met during courtship. This does not necessarily mean that they have changed; rather, you are now being introduced to that part of them you never knew. Don't forget that we all put our best foot forward in courtship. Let's be honest— most couples would never have gotten married if they had known everything about each other at the beginning.

THE ABCD OF MARRIAGE—

- **A**vailability,
- **B**elievability,
- **C**onnectivity, And
- **D**ependability

Availability—You need to be available to your spouse. You should never be missing in action when your spouse needs you. Make your marriage a priority after God. Attend to your spouse's need promptly, and be an active participant in the day-to-day running of your household.

Believability—Believe in each other no matter what. Believe that you both have the ability to be better and to support each other in a manner that would make you better. Be true to your word. Let your yes be simply yes and your no be simply no. Your word should never be secondguessed. You are your word, and your word is you. Do not make light of what you say and do. A white lie is still a lie. Create an environment where you can earn your spouse's trust. Believe that together you can overcome whatever comes your way.

Connectivity—Connect with your spouse spiritually, emotionally, and physically. Stay connected no matter what comes your way. You cannot afford to disconnect at any time, as this can lead to separation. The essence of connecting spiritually, emotionally, and physically is to promote oneness and build a lasting marriage. So find ways to stay connected to your spouse.

Dependability—Your spouse must be able to depend on you no matter what. You must be trustworthy. It is of the utmost importance that you keep your word and do what you said you will do. Go where you say you are going, and if plans change along the way let your spouse know. Your spouse should be able to trust you to do the right thing whether or not he or she is there with you.

Exercise: Take turns to ask each other the following questions:

1. What can I do to make your life better?

2. How can I better connect with you?

3. What things are important to you that I have overlooked?

CHAPTER SIX

Stages of Marriage

We are designed by God to adapt, and God-made married couples should be adapters. When God blessed both male and female after creation, His blessing included the ability to be adapters. Every human being possesses the ability to adapt. We may choose not to adapt, but we all have the ability to adapt.

American electronics runs on 110 voltage, while Europeans electronics run on 220 voltage. What allows you to use your gadgets in countries with different voltages is an adapter. Likewise, when storms of life show up or circumstances changes, couples in a God-made marriage are able to adapt and overcome. Do not run, do not leave, do not give up—stay and adapt. The word of God is an adapting tool, so use it as needed. Please note that you are not to adapt to any kind of abuse, as you were not designed by God to be abused. A God-made marriage is an abuse-free marriage.

Marriage is in stages, and every stage is necessary. There are important lessons to be learned in each stage, so you cannot skip any stage. Learning to adapt through the experiences of each stage will make your marriage stronger.

STAGE ONE: THE NEWLYWED STAGE

The newlywed stage is fun and exciting. You are overjoyed with being Mr. & Mrs. The sky is blue, the grass is green. The person is just perfect for you. Everything is perfect. You are over the moon at this stage. You are in love and you probably sang Louis Armstrong's "What a Wonderful World" repeatedly. You are pleasant to each other, and you go all out to please the one you love. You look your best, you wear your best, and you give your best to each other. You cheerfully do things for each other and will sacrifice everything for the love of your life. Everything looks and sounds good; everything smells and taste good. Your love for each other at this stage is extravagant, and you do not care who sees it or what they have to say about it. You feel elated with the opportunity to do for each other, and always look to please each other. The average life span of the newlywed phase is one to three years.

STAGE TWO: THE POSTEXCITEMENT STAGE

Once the excitement and the surge of emotions is over. When the fervor of being married fades and you settle down into your new life, most couples begin to

60

experience problems, and they disagree on issues more frequently, issues you might have seen at the first stage but chose to ignore, or issues that were just unseen at the beginning. As we said earlier, most people put their best foot forward and are good at selling themselves when looking for a life partner. This is just so you will like and buy the "product." Men and women say the right things and do the right things. They seem just perfect. But after the blissful period wears off, they begin to discover each other's flaws.

Lara

In my case, Henry would sing to me every night on the phone, and he sounded great. But after we got married, I realized he was a terrible singer. He could not hold a single note. He was so terrible I had to tell him to stop singing. I could not understand what was happening. Why did this man who used to serenade me to sleep with his perfect baritone voice sound like this now?

Then one day Henry answered my question and said: "You were in love and heard what you wanted to hear." I am sure you can think of many things that looked right and sounded right at first but were not so afterward.

You probably told yourself she was the best cook and later found out she hates to boil water, let alone cook a meal. Or he was such a gentleman and would not let you lift a finger without offering to help, but now you cannot get him off the couch to put his cup in the sink, let alone wash the dishes. Like Henry would often say, "After we got married, Lara let her cats out of the bag and I let mine out. Then I realized her cats were white and mine were black."

This is the stage where you each start to introduce your real self to the other without saying, "This is who I am." Based on your actions, your spouse gets to meet the side of you that he or she never bargained for. You enter a state of reality and start to ask yourself, "Who is this person here, and where is the person I married?" Problems, arguments, and disagreements seem to be the order of the day. Wedlock starts to look like a deadlock. You ask yourself over and over again, "What have I done? Why did I get married? Can I really spend the rest of my life with this person?" You tell yourself, "I didn't pray enough, I didn't hear God, I wasn't thinking clearly." Then you finally tell yourself, "My parents were right. I made a huge mistake and married the wrong one."

This cycle of negative thoughts, if not stopped, can convince you that you are not in love with your spouse. Many quit on their marriages at this stage.

Please understand that love is more than a feeling—it is a choice that requires action at different stages. When you said, "I do," you made a choice to be there through the good, the bad, and the ugly. So get rid of your all-or-nothing thinking and your tendency to see things in absolute black or white categories. This phase is normal and it will pass. So separate your thoughts from your feelings, and stop focusing on the negative parts of your marriage. The sooner you recognize this stage in your marriage and treat it as such, the quicker it is to move to the next level.

"So, what do I do now?"

We are glad you asked. You go to stage three.

STAGE THREE: THE "GETTING TO KNOW YOU, GETTING TO KNOW ALL ABOUT YOU" STAGE

Couples come into marriage with ideas about how it is supposed to work. It is obvious at this point that your spouse is clearly not the person you married, and the reality is different from your expectations. This is the stage where you begin to separate facts from fiction.

Since you do not fully know who you married, you should not be disappointed, but rather take time to know and understand your spouse and grow through your differences. Discover what pleases your spouse and what irritates your spouse. Know what your spouse likes and do it, and do not do whatever your spouse dislikes.

It will require you to study your spouse and ask questions. You must first be a student learning about your spouse, and in time you will become an expert. Be intimately acquainted with your spouse in all aspects of love. Pay attention to small details. Ignoring small details can have big ramifications.

Lara

At this stage, I found out that Henry actually disliked the things I thought he liked. I used to cook a lot with onions and garlic, only to find out he hated them. I was so sure he was a movie person like me because we went to the movies very often, only to find out he went because of me. Well, that explains why he fell asleep at every movie.

Be prepared to accept that you may have been wrong about several things all along, and be willing to make changes immediately. You may have convinced yourself that he enjoys your cooking more than his mother's, only to find out otherwise. Take time to know your spouse. Most wives do better jobs of knowing their husbands than the husbands do knowing their wives. That is why the Bible recommends in 1 Peter 3:7 that husbands dwell with their wives "according to knowledge." It means to take time to know her and understand her.

We once heard a story about a man who found a genie lamp while walking along the shore. When the genie said he could grant him one wish, the man asked that the genie should build him a bridge from San Francisco to Hawaii so he could drive there whenever he wanted. The genie, shocked at the request, said, "Do you know how much concrete and time it will take to build a bridge from here to Hawaii? Ask for something else." Then the man said, "I would like to know and understand my wife very well, so grant that wish instead." The genie replied, "Let's go back to the bridge wish. Is it a two-lane or four-lane bridge you want?"

We know it is easier said than done, but it is possible for husbands to know and understand their wives. We assure you that you will learn something new about her daily. Like why she tries on dresses that are two sizes smaller than her actual size and acts surprised when it does not fit, or why she tries on several shoes at several shoe stores only to go back and buy the first shoes she tried on several hours earlier at the first shoe store. This is probably a good time to recite the Serenity Prayer before you read further:

God, grant me the serenity to accept the things I cannot change, The courage to change the things I can, And the wisdom to know the difference. Amen.

Henry

The evidence of your love for your spouse is your ability to make changes when needed. Notice I said "your ability to make changes," not "your quest to change your spouse."

You have read that the first year of our marriage was very rough. I kept asking God to change Lara, because I was convinced she was the problem and the one who needed to change. Little did I know that she was also asking God to change me, because she was convinced I was the problem and the one who needed to change. We were each praying hard to convince God to change the other.

But nothing happened until I was humble enough

to stop asking God to change her and began to ask Him to help me make the changes in myself I needed to make. I immediately started to see areas I needed to work on, and as I began to change I started to see changes in Lara as well. It is important to acknowledge and keep track of these changes when they occur. You should also affirm the positive changes your spouse makes when you notice them.

STAGE FOUR: THE DIRECTION "I CAN SEE CLEARLY NOW THE RAIN IS GONE" STAGE

At this stage you now have a better understanding of your spouse, and you have a clearer picture of your marriage. You have separated facts from fiction and have come to accept the person you married. Now it's time for you to agree on the direction you both will be heading in. You may not be able to agree on everything at first, but start with the basics. It is important that you both are headed in the same direction.

Can two people walk together without agreeing on the direction? — Amos 3:3 (NLT)

Putting things in order will help you as you both head in the same direction. "Order" is putting things where they belong. For example, you don't think about buying a car when you do not have a job. Having a car is good, but the job comes before the car. Marriage is a journey with several turns; therefore, agreeing on the direction is imperative to move forward.

STAGE FIVE: THE BONDING STAGE (. . . AND THE TWO SHALL BECOME ONE FLESH)

Too many couples quit on their marriage before the bonding phase. This is the stage where you truly become one. You are a team, and you are secure in knowing that you have each other's backs. Empathy becomes the fundamental way of being together. This is a stage where you put yourself in your spouse's shoes. It requires heart work in order to bond and to keep the marriage alive. This is the rewarding stage of oneness, comfort, common interests, unity, support, security, and teamwork. Although disagreements may still arise, they are not seen as the end but merely as bumps along this lifelong journey of marriage. We will discuss bonding further in the next chapter. The proof of love in marriage is the willingness to be one

STAGE SIX: THE FRIENDSHIP STAGE

Friendship is a very important component in the preservation of marriage. Most relationships that leads to marriage often start with friendship. Friendship creates an environment of comfort and safety where grievances can be addressed without animosity. Stay friends no matter what, as this will help you foster healthy emotions toward each other. Your spouse should be your best friend for life. Your friendship provides access to your spouse's intimate opinion on issues you would not comfortably discuss with other people. You become each other's closest confidant, which creates a strong bond between you. This bond will keep you together through the good, the bad, and the ugly times. When married couples are friends, their marriage is less susceptible to breakups, and they can overcome challenges together.

Friends love through all kinds of weather, and families stick together in all kinds of trouble. — Proverbs 17:17 (MSG)

STAGE SEVEN: THE MATURING STAGE

The maturing stage is where, much more than the two becoming one, you become each other's lifeline. Having gone through the previous stages, there is a great display of tender love and care in the maturing stage. The value of intimacy with your spouse far outweighs the gratification of sex. This stage is evident in older married couples because they have been married for a long time and have shared experiences. The marriage vow is so vivid, you are partners for life and only death can separate you at this stage. The time it takes to get to this stage varies with each couple.

Exercise: Take turns to ask each other the following questions

1. What stage would you say we are at in our marriage? Why?

2. What issues are important to you in this stage of our marriage?

3. If we could improve three areas of our marriage, what would they be?

CHAPTER SEVEN

Romance and Lovemaking

Certainly—but only within a certain context. It's good for a man to have a wife, and for a woman to have a husband. Sexual drives are strong, but marriage is strong enough to contain them and provide for a balanced and fulfilling sexual life in a world of sexual disorder. The marriage bed must be a place of mutuality—the husband seeking to satisfy his wife, the wife seeking to satisfy her husband. Marriage is not a place to "stand up for your rights." Marriage is a decision to serve the other, whether in bed or out. Abstaining from sex is permissible for a period of time if you both agree to it, and if it's for the purposes of prayer and fasting—but only for such times. Then come back together again. Satan has an ingenious way of tempting us when we least expect it. I'm not, understand, commanding these periods of abstinence—only providing my best counsel if you should choose them. —1 Corinthians 7:2–6 (MSG)

When God established marriage, He had intimacy

as the nucleus of marriage when He declared "and the two shall be one." Lovemaking is a wonderful gift from God to married couples, so enjoy it. Lovemaking is different from sex, and it is important that you understand the difference. Too many couples are just having sex instead of making love, and the result is lack of intimacy. Sex is a quick act intended to satisfy your sexual hunger. It is mostly about quantity rather than quality. Lovemaking, on the other hand, is a spiritual affair and is about you pleasuring your spouse; therefore, it cannot be rushed. It is slow, sensual, and fulfilling. Lovemaking is going on an ecstatic adventure of a lifetime exploring and discovering new ways to use your God-given tools to express passionate love to each other. Lovemaking is all about quality, as it affects every part of your body and soul. Quick sex is okay from time to time, but you need to spend quality time making love to each other often. We recommend that you check into a hotel for an overnight stay a couple of times a year just to make love and pleasure each other without any interruption from the outside world.

Sexercise has so many benefits. It will lower your cholesterol, boost your immunity, improve your heart health, relieve your stress, ease your anxieties, boost your brain power, and promote good sleep. Romance is a process that leads to good lovemaking, so no day should go by without you meaningfully touching, romantically kissing, and lovingly hugging each other.

Never stop doing the good things you enjoyed doing together when you first met. You were romantic at the beginning of your marriage—do not stop now. You wore silky lingerie to bed at the beginning of the marriage, now you wear old T-shirts and sweatpants to bed. You showered and smelled nice every night before coming to bed, now you come to bed with the smell from your job.

Henry

I remember when Lara and I were in courtship, we enjoyed spending time together. I would pick her up from her place and we would go for long rides, see good movies, have dinners, dance, laugh and go places together. When I took her back to her place at the end of the day, there were always long moments of silence, because she didn't want to be without me and I didn't want to be without her. When we got married, we never stopped catching good movies even though I sometimes sleep half way through. Despite our busy schedule, we never stopped dancing, laughing, taking long rides and having fun. Only this time I get to take her home with me and continue the fun.

Do not stop being romantic and intimate with each other. And please do not reserve this for special occasions only. It does not have to be expensive. Wives put more effort into romance than the husbands, and it should not be so. There are so many inexpensive things you can do with your wife that will melt her heart and lead to a superb night of lovemaking. Send flowers, chocolates, or lunch, just because. Take her for a walk.

Plan a date night, even if it is to Boston Market, just so she does not have to cook dinner. Go share a dessert and drinks at a restaurant. Take her to an ice cream parlor. Go watch a movie at the theatre. Go shopping with her and watch her try on several clothes and shoes. Window shop at the mall and grab something to eat. Drive to the beach or a quiet spot, sit in the backseat of your car, and watch a movie on your tablet with drinks and snacks.

Husband, celebrate your wife and treat her like royalty, a queen, a superstar. Hold the door for her, hold her hands, pull out her chair, put on and take off her coat, pour her drink, rub her feet, run her bathwater, give her a full body massage, cook dinner. Call or text her during the day so she knows that you still have her in mind. Pick her up from work sometimes. Pick up a small gift for her to show how much you appreciate her. Never forget her birthday or your wedding anniversary. Save those important dates on your cell phone, yearly reminders, or chat boxes.

Wife, treat your husband like royalty, a king, a superstar. Meet him at the door and kiss him like you have not seen him in months. Take baths and shower together. Have a candlelit dinner on your living room floor. Wear silk nightgowns to bed often, not "the fabric of our lives." Invest in some sexy underwear and a negligee. Look good at home, not just when you go out. Catwalk in heels and some jewelry, and then roleplay. Play some sexy bedroom games. Turn off the lights, light some candles, turn on the music, and see where it takes you. This is what romance is all about. Keep passion alive by making things fun and exciting in your marriage.

Note that you may not always feel intensely romantic and loving toward each other due to the busyness of life and stress. Stress is a killer of romance. When you are both stressed, you will take out your frustrations on each other. Sometimes stress will make you feel like you are no longer in love with each other. What is stressful for the husband may not be so for his wife, and vice versa. Work may be the source of his stress, while running the home may be the source of her stress. Stress is stress and should never be trivialized, so do not consider your stress greater than your spouse's. Discern the source of your stress and deal with it. Heed to the warning signs of stress and do what is necessary to alleviate it.

It is important to balance work and play. Take time to rest at the end of each day and workweek. Soak in the bathtub with candlelights, some soap petals, soft music, and your favorite drink. Relax and watch a good movie, catch up on your favorite television shows, or read a book. If you both cannot do this at the same time, then take turns to relax while the other watches the children, or get a babysitter. Put a Do Not Disturb sign on the door if you have to or tell the children you are on time-out,—like we told our boys, who loved that their parents had time-outs, too.

Be happy, yes, rejoice in the wife of your youth. Let her breasts and tender embrace satisfy you. Let her love alone fill you with delight. —Proverbs 5:18–19 (TLB)

Find time to sustain your love life by spending meaningful and enjoyable time together. Text each other sweet nothings during the day that will lead to an amazing night. Have frequent date nights, go on weekend getaways, go to marriage retreats like our "God-made marriage retreat," go on vacations together. Couples that are thriving in their marriage will tell you that the intentional time they spend together talking, laughing, playing, and enjoying each other's company is what sustains their love.

Couples do tend to see a decline in romance, especially during the early years of raising their children, because their attention is focused on the children. However, it is important that you do not neglect each other or stop doing the things that you both love. If your spouse is disconnecting or you see a decline in sex and intimacy, never assume—ask why, and be ready to listen without judging and make changes as needed. Do not let your smell change from perfume to baby formula permanently. Do not stay in your pajamas all day. You were together before the children, and they will grow up and leave you in no time. So do not make your marriage all about your children. Spend quality time together doing what you both like. All these things will help keep romance alive in your marriage.

DEEP INTIMACY

Lack of Intimacy is one of the reasons couples break up. Over the years, we have had married people express feelings of loneliness and disconnection from their spouses. A common complaint was lack of intimacy, spiritually, emotionally, and sexually. Intimacy in marriage is spiritual and emotional commitment that is expressed through physical affection, sexual pleasure, and complete transparency between partners at the highest level. Spiritual, emotional, and sexual intimacies are all connected; therefore, you need a balance in all three areas to enjoy deep intimacy.

Intimacy is a viable component in a healthy marriage. Deep intimacy in marriage is not automatic or accidental. It requires intentional effort to start, takes time to build, commitment to maintain, and sacrifice to sustain. Deep intimacy will lead to a deeper understanding of your spouse. The more you connect with your spouse intimately, the better you will understand each other and empathize with each other.

When you are deeply intimate with your spouse, you will be able to sense what they are feeling or saying without words being uttered. You understand and support each other's goals and dreams. You will know each other's strengths and vulnerabilities at a deep level. Trust is built and never betrayed. You have utmost respect for each other. You gladly serve the needs of your spouse and often put your spouse's need before yours.

We could never understand how some people can be so respectful and nice to others but nasty and mean to their spouses. Nobody on earth deserves to be treated better than your spouse and children. Deep Intimacy provides inner access to the deeper feelings of your spouse that you might not have known prior to getting married. To be intimately acquainted with your spouse, you must start by acknowledging your spouse's feelings whenever they are expressed. The feelings a person expresses in marriage may not always be right, but they need to be acknowledged. If you ignore your spouse's expressed feelings over a period of time, it could lead to being disconnected intimately. The care and loving affection that you displayed before marriage moved you to say "I do." You both cannot ignore each other's expressed feelings whether they seem right or wrong to you. Your friendship will lead to deep intimacy.

Marriage was all God's idea, so you cannot leave Him out of the equation and expect it to work the way He intended. It is not by accident that you chose each other out of eight billion people on earth. God placed you together for a purpose, so you need Him for your marriage to work well. God and prayer are absolute necessities in a God-made marriage. A family that prays together consistently stays together consistently. So connect with God on a deeper level, and you will see the impact it will have on your marriage. Hold on to each other and never give up. Make sure you have each other's back no matter what. We have each other's backs and more importantly we know God has our backs.

EMOTIONAL INTIMACY

Emotional intimacy is the ability to openly share your feelings, strengths, weakness, and vulnerabilities with your spouse without any sense of guilt or shame.

We have drawn strength by reminiscing on the good old days during our pressured moments in life. In the early years of our marriage, our coworkers would ask for overtime just so they would not have to go home to their nagging spouses. we would turn down overtime so we could spend quality time with each other.

Marriage is a good place to build great memories. We have discovered that the intimate memories we have built in our marriage have been a source of strength for us, and they help us stay passionate.

When couples are emotionally intimate, they are secured in their love for each other and have unwavering trust for each other. When you are emotionally intimate with your spouse, you feel as if you can see into their soul, knowing their hopes, dreams, and fears, and understand them at a deep level. When couples connect emotionally, they can easily pick up when something is wrong with their spouse, even if no words are spoken.

Emotional intimacy does not happen automatically. You can be married for a long time and not be emotionally connected. It takes time and commitment to get to this level of emotional connection.

SEXUAL INTIMACY

Sexual drives are strong, but marriage is strong enough to contain them and provide for a balanced and fulfilling sexual life in a world of sexual disorder. The marriage bed must be a place of mutuality—the husband seeking to satisfy his wife, the wife seeking to satisfy her husband. Marriage is

not a place to "stand up for your rights." Marriage is a decision to serve the other, whether in bed or out.
—1 Corinthians 7:3–5 (MSG)

SOME FAULTY THINKING ON SEXUAL INTIMACY

• Intimacy is due to us having lots of sex. Intimacy begins in the heart, not during sex. It does not just happen because couples have sex. You may have sex and not be intimately acquainted with each other, but you cannot be intimately acquainted with each other without making love (unless illness or old age is a factor).

The lack of sexual intimacy is sometimes an indication of underlying issues in the marriage. It is unrealistic to expect that you will have hot and wild sex forever. Sexual desires will change with time for most couples, usually because of the busyness of life, low libido, age, or health issues. When sex life slows down drastically or becomes boring, or your marriage becomes sexless, you must be honest with each other and talk about it. Seek medical advice to determine how to reignite the passion.

• Watching pornography together helps spice things up. Pornography is ungodly, and it is toxic. Unfortunately, porn has become an epidemic even in marital homes. Reports shows that It is just as addictive as drugs or alcohol and is becoming the alternative for sexual gratification in marriages.

Watching porn does not spice things up; rather, it messes thing up. Lovemaking is meant to be enjoyed, and there are several ways to improve your enjoyment without it. If you open that door, it will poison your marriage and could eventually destroy your union. Intimacy is a sacred and private thing designed by God to be between a husband and his wife. You must honor your marriage and guard the sacredness of sexual intimacy between each other. Watching pornography is like bringing a third party into your sexual relationship with your spouse. Watching porn is an adulterous act, because you are getting sexual fulfillment from a third party.

Marriage is to be held in honor among all [that is, regarded as something of great value], and the marriage bed undefiled [by immorality or by any sexual sin]; for God will judge the sexually immoral and adulterous. —Hebrews 13:4 (AMP)

You cannot walk outside of the parameters God sets and expects your marriage to function properly.

TRANSPARENCY

Transparency is vital for deep intimacy to occur in a marriage. It is the level of maturity couples attain that enables them to simply be honest about everything. Transparency requires that we must be both trusting and trustworthy. There should be no secrets, no secret passwords, secret emails, secret cell phones, secret bank accounts, etc. Bear in mind that secrets never stay secrets forever. They will one day come out and could hurt your marriage. So be an open book and keep everything out in the open. There are no excuses for withholding the truth from your spouse. No matter what, tell the truth. Be mature enough to handle the truth you are told. Don't react, respond. Transparency brings things into the light and takes power out of the enemy's hand to divide you.

The institution of marriage also requires commitment, consistency, and contentment. It is through these processes that a husband and a wife will develop deep appreciation for each other and connect at a deeper level.

COMMITMENT

Marriage is a covenant relationship, so genuine commitment is required. "Commitment" is the state or quality of being dedicated to your marriage. It means staying true and loyal to your spouse. Feelings come and go, emotions rise and fall, but commitment stays the same.

I will never leave you nor forsake you. —Hebrews 13:5 (ESV)

Just as Christ, who is the embodiment of love, is committed to loving us despite our faults and failures, so also does love compel you to give your total commitment to your spouse, and this leads to deep intimacy with your spouse. True commitment is when we trust or yield ourselves totally to God and our spouse.

Our society needs more examples of couples that are committed to each other and are enjoying their longlasting marriages. No matter what you are going through, stay committed to making each other's lives better. Regardless of how many times you have been knocked down, get back up again and keep working on it. Get the help you need but stay committed. Any marriage can quickly become dysfunctional when it lacks commitment.

> *In marriage, love commits to the relationship and never gives up. Love goes all out and always desires to give. Love never fails.*

One of the enemies of commitment in marriage is lust. Lust makes you crave for what is beyond your reach and is never good for you. In marriage, love gives access to new ways of understanding for the betterment of the couple. You have access to the gifts and beautiful fruits of the spirit that God placed within your spouse. Nothing should be able to come between your love for each other, absolutely nothing. In marriage love commits to the relationship and never gives up. Love goes all out and always desires to give. Love never fails.

Husbands, go all out in your love for your wives, exactly as Christ did for the church—a love marked by giving, not getting. Christ's love makes the church whole. His words evoke her beauty. Everything He does and says is designed to bring the best out of her, dressing her in dazzling white

silk, radiant with holiness. And that is how husbands ought to love their wives. They're really doing themselves a favor—since they're already "one" in marriage. No one abuses his own body, does he? No, he feeds and pampers it. That's how Christ treats us, the church, since we are part of his body. And this is why a man leaves father and mother and cherishes his wife. No longer two, they become "one flesh."
—Ephesians 5:28–31 (MSG)

CONSISTENCY

Therefore, my beloved brethren, be steadfast, immovable, always abounding in the work of the Lord, knowing that your toil is not in vain in the Lord. —1 Corinthians 15:58 (NASB)

The success of any marriage is based on the consistency of both spouses. It is being in harmony with principles that unifies you. Be consistent in your marriage. Be romantic, not just on Valentine's Day. Be kind and good to your spouse, not just on special occasions. If you do the same thing you will get the same result. If you begin to see a different outcome, then you must trace your steps backward and see what you did differently. Be helpful to your spouse. Your consistency in loving and helping is never in vain.

CONTENTMENT

Contentment in a marriage is priceless. It is one of the best gifts you can have in your marriage. Contentment brings satisfaction, fulfillment, happiness, pleasure, cheerfulness, ease, comfort, serenity, and tranquility. Discontentment causes disappointment, disgruntlement, displeasure, unhappiness, and unthankfulness. Your discontentment adds unnecessary weight, stress, and pressure on your marriage and your spouse.

Not that I was ever in need, for I have learned how to be content with whatever I have.

I know how to live on almost nothing or with everything. I have learned the secret of living in every situation, whether it is with a full stomach or empty, with plenty or little. For I can do everything through Christ, who gives me strength.
—Philippians 4:11–13 (NLT)

We live in a time when more and more people are so discontent with their lives no matter where they are. They say, "I will be happy when I get married." "I will be happy when my spouse acts right." "I will be happy when I lose weight." "I will be happy when you get back your six-pack." "I will be happy when we have kids." "I will be happy when these children move out." "I will be happy when we buy a house." "I will be happy when the house is paid for." "I will be happy when we make more money." And the discontentment goes on.

Being content does not mean there is nothing more you want in life; it means you are happy and satisfied where you are on your way to where you are going. Sometimes in life, things take longer than you want them to, so you must decide to trust God on the way there. Ask God for great things in your marriage, but don't let it be a bother to you if you don't get it or if it is taking too long to come.

Please understand that your happiness and contentment is not based solely on your spouse making you happy. You make the choice to be happy and content. This is my take on the issue of contentment: Be happy "here" while on your way "there," because you can never ever get "there" until you are content, happy, and thankful for "here."

Exercise: Take turns to ask each other the following questions

1. Are you satisfied with our intimacy? If not, how can I make it better?

2. Do we have an honest and transparent relationship?

3. Do you trust me? If not, how can I earn your trust back?

CHAPTER EIGHT

Serving Each Other

"Here is a simple, rule-of-thumb guide for behavior: Ask yourself what you want people to do for you, then grab the initiative and do it for them. —Matthew 7:12 (MSG)

Marriage is teamwork. It takes two willing people to make any marriage work and run smoothly. The above scripture says it well: "Ask yourself what you want people to do for you, then grab the initiative and do it for them." Everything should be mutual in a God-made marriage. It is giving and taking, never one-sided. It is essential for couples to demonstrate mutual love and care, mutual bonding, mutual empathy, mutual respect, agreement, and mutual submission toward each other. This is God's plan for every marriage. Marriage is designed for mutual comfort, demonstrated by the giving of oneself for the betterment of your spouse. The success and the foundation of marriage can be found in the scripture above.

We all have our preconceived notions of marriage either from watching our parents or watching others. No two marriages are alike, but there are godly principles that will work in every marriage.

MUTUAL LOVE AND CARE

In a God-made marriage mutual love and care are required. Love and care is a two-way street where you strike a balance between giving and receiving it. Do not just receive love; give love back. Do not just receive care; you should care for your spouse too. Do not make excuses that you do not know how to love and care, learn it. You cannot just be a taker; you must be a giver as well. You should not take more than you give; you should rather give more than you take. Love and care should never be one-sided, otherwise you will wear out the giver. Expect arguments, resentments, and frustrations when the giver becomes worn out.

When our sons, Tosan and Viomo, were toddlers, they were very close and still are. They profess their love for each other often, but as soon as there is a disagreement, or one brother breaks the other's toy, they use their famous lines: "You are no longer my brother" or "I don't love you anymore." We have to settle their countless disputes and remind them that they will always be brothers. We also have to remind them that they still love each other, even though they may not like what just transpired. This happens several times a day. So one minute they say they are not brothers anymore or do not love each other, and the next minute they are hugging, laughing, and playing.

Likewise, when couples disagree on issues, it should not affect their love for each other. I am not saying to condone their behavior, but your love for each other should stay intact. There is no better way to describe love than the description in 1 Corinthians 13:4–7 (MSG):

Love never gives up.

Love cares more for others than for self.

Love doesn't want what it doesn't have.

Love doesn't strut,

Doesn't have a swelled head,

Doesn't force itself on others,

Isn't always "me first,"

Doesn't fly off the handle,

Doesn't keep score of the sins of others,

Doesn't revel when others grovel,

Takes pleasure in the flowering of truth,

Puts up with anything,

Trusts God always,

Always looks for the best,

Never looks back,

But keeps going to the end.

"Love does not keep score of the sins of others." Couples often complain and keep records of each other's wrongdoings. They pick and choose what memories to keep and what memories to discard. They remember the date, time, weather, even what clothing was worn. We hear comments like "I remember that day like it was yesterday. It was March 1, 1959. It was raining outside; you had on gray sweatpants and a light blue sweatshirt." Yet the same spouse would not remember what good deed was done a month ago. Stop remembering your past mistakes and choose to forget them. Learn from them, heal from them, and move on. Rehashing the past is like picking the scab off an old wound; it will never heal properly.

> *Stop remembering your past mistakes, choose to intentionally forget them. Learn from them, heal from them and move on.*

Rather than keeping scores of each other's wrongdoings, start keeping scores of each other's rightdoings in a box or diary. Start a book of memories to store up all the good memories of your marriage, and visit this memory collection from time to time. It will remind you of why you fell in love with each other and will inspire you to stay in love with each other. Your memories could include a picture of you having a wonderful time together, a promise that you made to each other, love notes, or a record of a special occasion.

Henry

As a former professional soccer player, I know the importance of keeping scores. Stats are used to determine how good a competitor a player is. What's true of the professionals and their stats is also true for marriage. Spouses ought to keep a record of each other's right doings, and retrieve and remember them from time to time. By so doing you will realize you have a Hall of Famer for a spouse, and it will spur you into doing a lot of good for each other. Lara and I reminisce a lot on our past good times, and it brings us closer each time.

MUTUAL BONDING

In a God-made marriage mutual bonding is required for the two to become one. Mutual bonding is deep internal soul closeness. Couples who fail to bond will experience feelings of loneliness and unfulfillment. The two of you must become one; one with each other and one with God. God is the only bonding agent that holds things together permanently. Much of the unnecessary tension we see in marriages stem from couple's unwillingness to bond and choosing to hold on to their individuality.

As we said earlier, the proof of love is the willingness to become one with your spouse. When we give our individuality to God in a marriage, He blends it with our spouse's until husband and wife become one. Storms will come, winds will blow, but your marriage will still be standing after the storms, the rain, and the wind. Excluding God as the bonding agent in your marriage is like fixing a leaking pipe with a duct tape. The problem with this is that duct tape does not fix anything permanently. It is a temporary fix, and sooner or later it will fall apart. Both spouses must bond with God, because the better you bond with God, the better you will bond with your each other.

MUTUAL EMPATHY

In a God-made marriage mutual empathy is essential. It is so important to mutually experience the thoughts, emotions and direct experience of your spouse. Without empathy a spouse may be physically close by and yet be disconnected, because they fail to empathize with their partner. If your spouse is constantly making comments like "You don't care about what I am going through," "You don't help me around this house," "I am married but I feel like I am a single parent because you don't help me with the kids," the relationship lacks mutual empathy, and it should be corrected immediately. Whenever you are faced with a negative situation I encourage you to try and put yourself in your spouse's shoes. Empathy is the understanding of your spouse's feeling, because you have either experienced it yourself or you can put yourself in your spouse's shoes.

Lara

When I was in labor having our son Tosan, Henry could not stop saying, "I'm sorry you are in so much pain." "I wish I could go through this pain instead of you." "This is it, no more babies." "I cannot bear to see you go through this again." But then we were back in the same hospital fifteen months later having another baby. Henry stayed up nights to take care of our sons, so I could get some sleep. I did not like that he stayed up all night because he had to go to work in the morning, but he still insisted on doing it. He was showing empathy. There are several ways you can show empathy to your spouse, and it starts with addressing the immediate needs, care, or concern of your spouse without dismissing their feelings.

MUTUAL RESPECT

Mutual respect is a powerful tool in a God-made marriage. Respect in a marriage should never be one-sided, as it is in some cultures. Having a disposition of high regard and honor for each other should be paramount regardless of the situation. You are a king-and-queen combination, so treat each other as such.

Who you love, you also respect and honor. Demonstrating respect for each other shows that you care about each other's feelings, which communicates love. Who you admire, you respect and treat well. Mutual respect goes a long way in a marriage.

Find out what respect means to your spouse. There may have been times when you misconstrued the actions of your spouse as disrespectful. Conversely, what you may not consider to be disrespectful may in fact be disrespectful to your spouse. You may not consider yelling while talking to your spouse as being disrespectful but your spouse does. Pointing or snapping your fingers, rolling your eyes, and making head movements may not be a big deal to you and yet be considered disrespectful by your spouse.

You should never resort to name calling in a marriage. Under no circumstance should you use profanity, period. It is a total disrespect. If you want to be respected, please make sure you give respect.

Love each other with genuine affection, and take delight in honoring each other. —Romans 12:10 (NLT)

MUTUAL TRUST

A strong foundation of mutual trust is imperative in a God-made marriage. When there is trust, there is safety and truth. No room for deception, as this will very quickly kill trust in your marriage. I cannot overemphasize the importance of not betraying your spouse's trust, as it is hard to earn back once it is lost. However, trust can be restored and rebuilt after it is lost, so give each other the chance to earn that trust back.

MUTUAL VALUE

Marriage adds value to you, so place value on each other and your marriage. Who you value, you honor; and what you value, you keep. Never take each other for granted. Never take your unique roles for granted. Don't just live day to day—enjoy your marriage and build a better life of value together.

MUTUAL AGREEMENT

In a God-made marriage mutual agreement is the state of being in one accord and harmony even when there are differences in opinion.

Can two people walk together without agreeing on the direction? —Amos 3:3 (NLT)

Collaboration is an essential component of your marriage. Work in collaboration with your spouse, not in competition. Never make any major decisions unless both of you are in agreement. The bulk of marital problems occur when both spouses do not agree on a matter, and one goes ahead to make the decision for both. Put that thing on hold until you both agree on it.

Mutual agreement is like a coin. There are three sides to a coin: the head, the tail, and the edge where both sides meet. Similarly, are three sides to every matter: yours, your spouse's, and the middle ground where you both meet and then agree. It means that you help your spouse see and understand what they don't see or understand. This is not to impose your will on the other spouse, but to help them see clearly and make the best decision for the family.

Of course, each spouse could make minor decisions like what to cook for dinner or when to go shopping, but one partner cannot make a major decision such as buying a house, relocating, or quitting a job unless both spouses join in agreement. From how to raise and discipline the children to how you budget and spend, there must be mutual agreement—only you must ensure that the mutual agreement does not violate God's principles.

MUTUAL SUBMISSION

A God-made marriage has mutual submission, which is setting aside what you think is good for you and choosing what is best for your marriage. It is choosing to yield and walk in unity with your spouse rather than asserting your own way.

On the highway, a yield sign indicates that each driver must be prepared to stop if necessary to let a driver on another approach proceed. A driver who stops or slows down to let another vehicle through has yielded the right of way to that vehicle to prevent a collision. Just as in traffic, failure to yield in your marriage will lead to conflicts that you may not be able to resolve. You must learn to yield to your spouse when it is in the best interest of the marriage.

"Submission" consists of the prefix "sub" and the word "mission." The prefix "sub" means "under," or "below," like in the words "submarine" and "subway." Therefore, "submission" in this context simply means we both come under or submit to the mission that is the best for the marriage.

Submitting yourselves one to another in the fear of God.
—Ephesians 5:21 (KJV)

The submission is always for the advancement of the marriage. It does not make you a doormat to be walked upon, because submission is not subjection. The power and beauty of mutual submission is that rank and entitlement go out the window and are replaced with love, a desire to serve each other, and humility. Submission does not mean you agree on everything. It is not weakness but strength under control.

Henry

Many decisions I have made that putt my wife and her ideas before mine were misconstrued by some as being weak. Submission does not make you a weak person. It shows that you are secure in who you are and can allow the spotlight to be placed on your spouse when it is better for the marriage or the mission at hand. Mutual submission implies we are in partnership.

I remember when Lara and I first decided to become Licensed Clinical Christian Counselors. We took the first class together, but we ran into some financial woes and could no longer continue together. She automatically thought she would be the one to drop out of class, because that was what was culturally acceptable: The submissive wife steps down for her husband.

Instead, I did something that was totally outside of our culture but biblically profound. I said, "You are better in class than I am, so go ahead and finish. When you complete your studies then I will go back and finish mine." I supported her every step of the way until she finished, and then I resumed my studies. That is love and submission.

If your spouse is better at managing the finances, then submit to it. If you are better at organizing, then your spouse should submit to it. It is for the betterment of the marriage. Failure to mutually submit to each other in a marriage will lead to conflicts, which can in turn lead to bigger problems.

Exercise: Take turns to ask each other the following questions.

1. Do you think we have a mutual relationship?

2. What are your favorite memories of us together?

3. What would you like us to do more of together?

CHAPTER NINE

Effective Communication

The number one root cause of most if not all problems in a marriage is failure to communicate effectively. When communication succeeds in a marriage, there is peace, fulfillment, understanding, teamwork, security, and longevity. On the other hand, when communication breaks down, every area of the marriage will be affected. Spouses often experience restlessness, fear, confusion, mistrust, isolation, rejection, or a sense of dissatisfaction, and they might seek solace in others.

Effective communication is the key to a successful God-made marriage. It improves the quality of the marital relationship, and it also helps maintain understanding within the marriage. We all have had times when the action of our spouse felt to us like they didn't care. Communication between couples are sometimes flawed by misunderstanding and misinterpretation. Too often the misunderstanding brought about by lack of effective communication can be misinterpreted as "You don't care about me."

Henry

The most eye-opening encounter in regard to communication in our marriage occurred within the first year. Lara complained so much about my anger and lack of patience toward her, and I would always respond by denying any wrongdoing because I could not see what I was doing wrong. This created some unhappiness in our marriage. On our first year anniversary, I sat her down and said, "Please write down everything you think I do wrong that causes pain or hurt to you." She did, and it was a long list. I was very angry at her long list and disagreed with most of what she had written down. A few days later I caught myself doing some of the things she had complained about, and I immediately apologized. From that day I worked on everything, and to the glory of God I have greatly improved in that area of our relationship.

Effective communication requires active listening. Scripture recommends in James 1:19 (NIV) that you "should be quick to listen, slow to speak and slow to become angry". You need to listen to your spouse. You have access to information about yourself that no other person will be able to tell you. You can also access ideas of what pleases your spouse. Share with your spouse things that please you. God did it with us. The Bible says, "without faith it is impossible to please God"

(Hebrews 11:6 NIV). God wants us to know what pleases Him. The Bible also says that we should be holy as our father in heaven is holy. What God likes to see us do is very well communicated through the Bible. You should also do likewise with your spouse.

Remember how you used to talk for hours nonstop before you got married? You cannot stop now; no matter what, you must keep talking. Failing to talk to each other whenever a situation arises in your marriage will allow abnormalities to set in, but if you talk about it and deal with it, then the issue will be resolved.

One spouse is usually a talker while the other is a nontalker. The talker should always encourage the nontalker to discuss issues rather than sweep them under the carpet. Jesus puts it this way: "Men ought to pray and not faint" (Luke 18:1). If you stop talking with God through prayer, you will faint in the day of adversity.

If you faint in the day of adversity, your strength is small.
—Proverbs 24:10 (NKJV)

To "faint" means to give up and quit your position in life; in this case, we are talking about marriage. When couples start "fainting" in their marriage relationship, oftentimes it is a result of communication breakdown. A husband and wife who live under the same roof and are not speaking to each other have unfortunately created an unhealthy environment in which issues can fester, and this can ultimately lead to bigger problems. You may not always agree, but you must always talk.

Effective communication in marriage leads to a stronger, lasting marriage; with it, we can successfully overcome any adversity that life throws our way. You cannot afford to faint whenever your marriage is faced with challenges; you both must always keep the lines of communication open.

Effective communication is talking, listening, and coming to a resolve. To effectively communicate with your spouse, listen when he or she is speaking. Listening is not saying yes to everything, but rather it is acknowledging what is being said and validating your spouse. We encourage reflective listening which is when you listen to your spouse and then repeat back what you have just heard to confirm understanding. "Coming to a resolve" means making an agreeable decision after hearing what your spouse had to say. Misunderstandings can be avoided, and a lot can be accomplished when you effectively communicate.

Sometimes what you desire for your marriage may not be what is best for your marriage; therefore, you must be willing to talk with your spouse about the situation. Effective communication is not enforcing your opinion or will, nor is it winning an argument. It is coming to an agreement with what is best for the marriage. When one spouse is speaking, the other should be listening. When you listen, do not rush to say what you think you should say or what you have been dying to say. Instead, listen carefully to what your spouse is saying; if he or she is making a complaint, make an emotional connection with his or her plight. Be mindful of what you say and how you say it, because your words are powerful. You can use the same words under different circumstances and they will bring about a completely different outcome. Words can hurt or they can encourage your spouse, they can build up or they can tear down the marriage.

A kind answer soothes angry feelings, but harsh words stir them up. —Proverbs 15:1 (CEV)

How it is said is as important as what is said, so do not make excuses for talking rudely or harshly. Proper communication skills can be learned, and comments such as "You know this is how I talk" should stop. Do not be rigid or set in your ways. You can change for the better. Change is necessary sometimes, and it is good. Be willing to change, because change is inevitable, and it is constant. Recalibrate yourself, renew your mind, and get a new attitude.

Jesus demonstrated what effective communication is in the garden of Gethsemane. He was willing to put aside a desire to protect those He loved. He desired not to go to the cross—"if it is possible, let this cup pass from Me" (Matt. 26:39 NASB)—but after communicating with the Father, He chose to go with God's perfect plan, and His desire gave way to the response "Not my will but thine be done" (Luke 22:42 KJV). Likewise, when couples communicate effectively, their response to each other should be to consider what is best for the marriage.

Effective communication requires both spouses to know and understand each other's communication styles. Husbands and wives communicate differently. Most wives can articulate feelings better than their husbands can. I am sure you can think of several instances when you and your spouse spoke differently, and one did not understand the other. During those times when you may not fully understand what your spouse is saying, remember this does not mean they are wrong; it just means that we hear and process things differently. We think differently, we process things differently, and we understand differently. With this in mind, try listening to the words that are spoken by your spouse and hear what they are actually trying to say.

Lara

We were visiting friends house one time. During our conversation, the husband came across as loud, disrespectful, and condescending to his wife. His wife just smiled and responded so nicely each time. While we were puzzled by the way he spoke, his wife apologized and explained that he talks that way when he is passionate about what he is saying. She understood him and paid more attention to what he was saying rather than to how he was saying it. I brought the issue up on our way home, and Henry said, "It works for them because she understands him."

But if I don't understand the language that someone is using, we will be like foreigners to each other. —1 Corinthians 14:11 (CEV)

When one spouse is talking the other spouse is listening, processing, and understanding what is being said. Take time to fully understand what you're hearing before you respond. Repeat what was said to confirm you heard your spouse correctly, and ask questions when you hear something you are not familiar with. Never assume and do not jump to conclusions without hearing all your spouse has to say. Resolve the matter after both spouses have taken turn to listen, process, and understand what was said.

You cannot talk at the same time or try to outtalk the other spouse. Avoid yelling at each other. If you are both talking at the same time, then no one is listening. If no one is listening, the issue stays unresolved.

Have you wondered why you have been having disagreements on the same issue for years and it just does not go away? This is because it has not been resolved. Unresolved issues never go away; they stay around for as long as it takes to resolve them. Don't stay stuck on one issue for too long—work on resolving it quickly, so you can move on to other things.

Lara

I cannot begin to tell you how many times I have messed up in this area. I was the quick talker, so I would have my answers ready before Henry would finish saying whatever he had to say. And like a loaded machine gun, I would fire until I had used up all the bullets. When you fire shots, people will get hurt.

God-Made Marriage

There is one who speaks rashly like the thrusts of a sword, but the tongue of the wise brings healing. —Proverbs 12:18 (AMP)

Words hurt and cut deep. Once they are spoken they cannot be taken back, so be careful what you say, even when you are angry. Do not hurt each other with words. Our words should bring healing, not hurt.

How do you resolve any issue? By simply letting the word of God take precedent over what you think and how you feel. Allow God to have the last say in the matter. As Henry says, "God's word is my first priority and my final authority." Sharp words won't do it; your spouse will simply learn how to put you on mute—that is, even though your mouth is moving you will not be heard. The next time the same matter resurfaces, communicate effectively and it will pack its bag and leave your home. Just make sure you do not let it back in after it leaves.

Listening is a very important part of communication. It is the ability to accurately receive and interpret what your spouse is saying. It is being able to process and understand what your spouse is saying even if it is not said the right way. This again does not in any way excuse a spouse who refuses to learn to speak in a proper tone and manner. You have heard people say, "It is not what is said that matters but how it is said." We believe how it is said matters as much as what is being said.

A soothing tongue [speaking words that build up and encourage] is a tree of life, but a perversive tongue [speaking

104

words that overwhelm and depress] crushes the spirit.
—Proverbs 15:4 (AMP)

Remember when you were courting, you were very careful with your words. You were mindful of not only what you said but also of how you said it. This attitude should continue in your marriage. Pay attention to your mouth, because what comes out of the mouth of both spouses is very crucial. You cannot take back words after it is spoken. So be very careful what you say to each other even when you are angry. Anger is no justification for saying mean and hurtful things. The effect of your words will still linger long after they were spoken.

Words are powerful. Words can build up and words can tear down. One word can change a sentence completely. "Always" and "Never," for example, are words that often come up when couples disagree. "You always do this to me." "You never listen to me." "You never treat me right." "You always ruin the moment." "You are never around." "You always put other people before me." "You never appreciate anything I do." You can probably come up

> *If you are both talking at the same time, then no one is listening. If no one is listening the issue will stay unresolved. Unresolved issues never go away, they stay around for as long as it takes to resolve them.*

with many more on your own. An argument often ensues whenever those two words are used in this manner. Avoid such situations as much as you can.

Many think a thermometer and a thermostat are the same, but they are not. A thermometer registers the temperature of whatever environment it is placed in. So if you put it in a pot of boiling water the mercury will rise, and if you put it in cold water it will drop. The thermostat on the other hand, controls the temperature inside regardless of what is going on outside. So if it is set to seventy degrees, the room will stay at a comfortable seventy degrees even if the temperature is zero degrees outside.

Both of you should be like the thermostat, in control and regulated regardless of the issue at hand. Do not act like a thermometer that rises high and drops low with every matter. You must control yourself—your emotions, your actions, your thoughts, and your words.

We get it wrong nearly every time we open our mouths. If you could find someone whose speech was perfectly true, you'd have a perfect person, in perfect control of life. A bit in the mouth of a horse controls the whole horse. A small rudder on a huge ship in the hands of a skilled captain sets a course in the face of the strongest winds. A word out of your mouth may seem of no account, but it can accomplish nearly anything—or destroy it!

It only takes a spark, remember, to set off a forest fire. A careless or wrongly placed word out of your mouth can do that. By our speech we can ruin the world, turn harmony to chaos, throw mud on a reputation, send the whole world up in smoke and go up in smoke with it, smoke right from the pit of hell. This is scary. —James 3:2–7 (MSG)

Exercise: Take turns to ask each other questions #1 and #2, then do #3 together

1. Do I make you feel comfortable to express yourself freely and point out my mistakes?

2. Are there unresolved issues we need to address so we can move forward?

3. Practice reflective listening by listening to your spouse and then repeating back what you have just heard.

CHAPTER TEN

When Problems Arise

Healthy disagreements are an unavoidable part of every marriage. Problems will arise from time to time and for different reasons. You will sometimes see things from different vantage points.

IS IT A SIX OR A NINE? [6 OR 9]

Just because you see a six and your spouse sees a nine does not mean either of you are wrong. Try and see it from each other's perspective. There will be several times in your marriage when you will have differing viewpoints, and yet you will both be right. So instead of wasting time arguing about who is right and who is wrong, you should each try to see things from the other's perspective. Your marriage must be esteemed more highly than every issue you encounter.

When problems arise do not worry, because worrying will exponentially increase the problem.

Realize that things will not always go according to plan. Although it can be quite challenging to deal with all the variables that often take place when glitches happen in a marriage, it is however important not to point fingers during those moments. Instead, calm down and talk about the solution, not the problem. Resolve it and move forward. You have more ground to cover, don't stay too long on one issue. Focus on your future together, not the past mistakes. You can have disagreements without turning them into arguments, so do not throw jabs always remember you are on the same team.

Please know that the strength of your marriage will be tested. No matter what life deals you, learn to make the best of every situation. Weather storms together, and the things that would have brought you down or torn you apart will end up making you stronger than you were before. Troubled waters have over the years brought us together. This is possible in every marriage if both spouses are willing to allow God to take them through those tough times.

Do not assume the worst, as problems often seems worse than they usually are. No, it is not the end of your marriage, just another bump in the road. Talk about it with a soft and soothing voice. Listen to each other and validate what you are both saying. Learn to apologize when necessary, rather than pointing fingers at each other. Having your marriage right far outweighs you being right. God-made marriage is not "I'm right and you're wrong." Saying "I am sorry" does not make you weak; it is showing strength under control. Apologies are time-sensitive, so be quick to take responsibility for what you did wrong, apologize, and forgive each other. When you take too long to apologize, it loses its meaning. Pray about it. Praying has helped us during difficult situations in our marriage, so we recommend it. Always remember there is nothing you both and God cannot overcome in your marriage.

Make good use of touch control to calm the situation. Touch control is a powerful tool in calming people down. When couples are angry, they usually don't want their spouse to touch them when it is actually the best time to touch and be touched. Your touch is vital, especially during tense moments. Touch should be used to communicate love and affection. Our touch stimulates the release of neurological chemicals like oxytocin and serotonin that make us feel good, while also inhibiting chemicals that causes us to be stressed or tensed. So, during tense moments, use the power of touch to connect and calm each other down. Sometimes your touch alone can defuse the situation without words.

It is not just what you say or how you say it; it is also knowing when to say it. Good timing is crucial. The worst time to speak is when you are angry, so don't speak—just walk away to cool off. If your spouse walks away to cool off, please do not force the issue or insist on talking about the situation while things are still heated. You will have a better outcome if you give each other time to calm down and reflect after a disagreement.

Go ahead and be angry. You do well to be angry—but don't use your anger as fuel for revenge. And don't stay angry.

111

God-Made Marriage

Don't go to bed angry. Don't give the Devil that kind of foothold in your life. —Ephesians 4:26–27 (MSG)

Do not to go to bed angry at each other but know that not all problems can be resolved before bedtime. The Bible says not to go to bed angry, but it doesn't say every matter can be resolved before bedtime. Sleeping over a matter may produce a better outcome than trying to tackle it the same day. Learn to respond and not react to life's situations. Letting your spouse walk away to calm down is responding, while forcing your spouse to talk right there and then because you want a resolution is reacting. The reality is spouses deal with the problems and pressures of life differently. You may be immersed in what you are going through and fail to see that your spouse is also going through it and probably having it worse than you. You both need to be there for each other during those times. There are moments when all your spouse need is a space to think or to calm down, a listening ear, a hug, or a kiss. Be sensitive to know those moments and respond correctly. If you are not able to resolve a major issue on your own, then get help from someone with a proven track record of success in marriage counseling.

You can benefit from preventative marriage counseling as it will help improve your communication skills, better your love life, provide necessary tools for conflict resolution, and address unresolved issues before they become big problems. Do not wait until you are at the end of your rope to seek counseling. It should never be the last resort but a tool used to build a stronger and lasting marriage from the onset. We highly recommend that you both get counseling from a licensed counselor from time to time.

Forgiveness will play a major role whenever problems arise in your marriage. Choose to forgive past hurt without keeping scores. The past is past; don't hold on to it. Remember that love does not keep record of wrongdoings. You both have a lot ahead of you, so let go of the past and move forward. Do not be bitter, either; the same energy you use to be bitter can be used to better your marriage. No matter what may have happened, allow healing to take place. Healing starts with forgiveness. Forgive each other's past so you can heal and then reach for the future together.

I am still not all I should be, but I am bringing all my energies to bear on this one thing: Forgetting the past and looking forward to what lies ahead. —Philippians 3:13 (TLB)

Like a computer you must periodically scan for threats and viruses in your marriage as they can slow you down, create big problems, or destroy your marriage. A virus can be a person (or people) who constantly throws burning arrows, sows discord between you and your spouse, or brings their negative energy into your marriage. You must get rid of such people and extinguish their flaming arrows before they burn down your home. We have had to keep such people at bay, and it has been one of the best decisions we have made in our marriage.

Exercise: Do the following

1. Hold each other and look into each other's eyes without speaking for three minutes.

2. Ask each other: "What do we disagree the most about, and how can we resolve the problem?"

3. Say to each other: "Please forgive me for all the times I have hurt you with my words and actions."

CHAPTER ELEVEN

Identifying Your Uniqueness and Reconciling Your Differences

Oh yes, you shaped me first inside, then out; you formed me in my mother's womb. I thank you, High God—you're breathtaking! Body and soul, I am marvelously made! I worship in adoration—what a creation! You know me inside and out, you know every bone in my body; You know exactly how I was made, bit by bit, how I was sculpted from nothing into something. Like an open book, you watched me grow from conception to birth; all the stages of my life were spread out before you, The days of my life all prepared before I'd even lived one day. —Psalm 139:14-16 (MSG)

IDENTIFYING YOUR UNIQUENESS

The human body is by far the most complex and unique organism in the world. We are vastly complex and unique beings. The composition of every part of our body and the harmony of those parts together speak volumes about God. We are unique; no two human beings are alike. Even identical twins have their own uniqueness, which is usually how you can tell them apart. You must therefore appreciate each other's uniqueness as a couple. Don't try to change each other, allow God to do the changing through His Word.

Henry

Lara and I tried in the early years of our marriage to change each other. We each begged God to change the other, and nothing happened until one day I asked God to change me. As I began to change, I began to see changes in Lara also. We are like night and day, yet we make it work. We are now so thankful that we are different.

RECONCILING YOUR DIFFERENCES

Now the LORD God said, "It is not good (beneficial) for the man to be alone; I will make him a helper [one who balances him—a counterpart who is] suitable and complementary for him." —Genesis 2:18 (AMP)

God made us different on purpose and for a purpose. He never intended for the husband and his wife to be the same. The above scripture clearly states that the wife is a counterpart of her husband. A counterpart is someone holding a position or performing a function that corresponds to that of another person as well as complementing the other. You are the opposite of each other. The husband was created but the wife was formed. "To create" means to make something out of nothing, while "to form" is to make something out of an already existing thing. So, when God wanted to make Eve, all He did was take a rib out of the already existing Adam and formed Eve with it. We were made differently. The male and female anatomy are different in so many ways. Their skeletal structures are different. Their physical, mental, and emotional chemistries are different.

You are made differently: you think differently, you act differently, you talk differently, and you love differently. Most problems in marriages occur because we do not allow our spouse to be different. Do not try to change your spouse or force your spouse to conform to your ideas. Those forced changes can either improve or imprison your spouse and make them unhappy. We are different. Even our needs are different. What a man needs the most is respect and sex. What a woman need the most is love and security.

You are probably wondering why God would make a husband and his wife opposite of each other. Notice that a counterpart is described as having a function that corresponds. You are not in competition with each other. Because we are made differently, you must throw out the "anything you can do I can do better" attitude. God made the wife to have qualities, attributes, and responsibilities that corresponds to that of her husband so they will always need each other. Our frustrations ended the day we got this revelation that we are two completely different people yet made to complement each other.

Being different is not a bad thing, it is just different. You did not fall in love with only what you had in common, you fell in love mostly with what was different. Your difference is what attracted you to each other in the first place and should not tear you apart now. Perhaps you are quiet, she is opinionated. You are strong-willed, she has a gentle spirit. You are impatient, she is patient. You are organized, she is not. You are a night person, she is a day person. You like steak, she likes chicken. You like to be outdoors, she likes to be indoors. The point is, you are two different people, and you need to accept that your spouse is not you.

You are probably saying right now, "You don't know my spouse" or "You don't know how difficult my spouse is." You are right; I don't know, but God does. So talk to God to change your negative perception of your spouse. It is easier to see your spouse's fault than your own, so your frustration will be toward your spouse and not yourself. Does this mean neither of you can change when it is needed? Absolutely not. The proof that you love each other is your willingness to change for the better. However, you will have to come to terms with the fact that there are certain things your spouse will probably never change no matter how hard you try.

This is probably another good time to recite the serenity prayer.

God, grant me the serenity to accept the things I cannot change, The courage to change the things I can, And the wisdom to know the difference. Amen.

Lara

Accept your differences. I am always alarmed when I hear about couples filing for a divorce on the grounds of irreconcilable differences, when in most cases it was their differences that attracted them to each other in the first place. Over the years of counseling married couples both young and old, the one thing that is prevalent across the board is that most couples stop celebrating and respecting their differences. You can be different and still agree. "Irreconcilable differences" is a choice couples make when they refuse to agree. You cannot work or walk together unless you choose to agree. Thank God Henry and I are different. It is our differences that makes our marriage special.

Henry

Before we got married, Lara and I went almost everywhere together, did many things together, from church to social gatherings we were inseparable. But during the first year of marriage, the first thing I discovered was that I am a night person and Lara is a day person. I stay up late to pray, read, or watch television and study. Lara is the complete opposite; she goes to bed early and would not stay awake to pray with me at midnight. Back then I took offense to Lara's inability to stay up late to mean she was uncaring, unspiritual, and disrespectful. I misinterpreted the difference in her internal body clock as her inability to care about what mattered to me.

Differences should never be viewed as a spouse's insensitivity to the needs of the other, because it could be damaging to your marriage relationship. When you take your spouse's differences as inabilities, your failure to talk about the differences can trigger an emotional disengagement. Whenever you have different views and opinions, meet on common ground and help each other understand and see what the other may not see or understand. Some of your differences are actually good and can be reconciled. Celebrate your differences with respect and love toward each other, honoring God in your marriage.

Remember that your children are watching you and forming lasting opinions on love, commitment, how to relate with the opposite sex, and marriage based on what they see you do. Give them the confidence and assurance they need. Make them look forward to getting married.

Let us not give up the habit of meeting together. . . . Instead, let us encourage one another. —Hebrews 10:25 (GNT)

We have said that marriage is not all about finding the right person; it is being the right person. A wife once said that she and her husband are the same in everything.

Therefore, if he falls into a ditch, she would jump in right after him. Another wife said, "No, if my husband falls into a ditch, I will fetch a rope or get help to pull him out." Which spouse are you?

This makes a difference as to how couples resolve issues. The wife who jumps after her husband into the ditch would be trapped with her husband in the ditch, jeopardizing their chances of surviving. What is true for this wife is also true for marriage. When conflicts arise, both spouses cannot be overly angry at the same time. Both cannot be wrong, because two wrongs will not make a right. Be like the spouse who was calm enough to get a rope and pull her husband out of the ditch. When you are angry or in disagreement, both spouses must be willing to calm down before things get out of hand.

> *But all things are from God, Who through Jesus Christ reconciled us to Himself [received us into favor, brought us into harmony with Himself] and gave to us the ministry of reconciliation [that by word and deed we might aim to bring others into harmony with Him]. It was God [personally present] in Christ, reconciling and restoring the world to favor with Himself, not counting up and holding against [men] their trespasses [but cancelling them], and committing to us the message of reconciliation (of the restoration to favor).*
> —2 Corinthians 5:18–19 (AMPC)

When you both understand your uniqueness, it becomes easier to embrace your similarities and differences. By doing so, you will create an environment that is conducive for marriage, and your love for each other will grow. You will be able to reconcile all that seems irreconcilable, something neither of you could have done on your own. Embracing your uniqueness and differences in marriage makes you stronger as a team and allows you to accomplish more a lot faster. However, these same differences can also lead to misunderstandings, conflicts, and problems unless they're properly worked out. The promise you made to each other that only death will separate you should never be broken regardless of your differences.

Marriage requires learning to embrace and reconcile the differences and, with time, mature through them. Learn to talk about your blessings more than your burdens. Do not be one of those couples who talk only about their marital woes. When you focus on the burdens, the value of your spouse and your marriage will depreciate in your eyes. Marriage should improve you and change you for the better. You don't change your spouse; marriage does.

Often in weddings you hear this phrase from the clergy or officiating person, "I now pronounce you husband and wife." This is attaching a new identity to the just-married couple, declaring that they are no longer singles and are now to live together as one in holy matrimony. Just like the Christian life, marriage provides couples with a new identity: "old things have passed away and all things have become new" (2 Cor. 5:17). With this new identity comes a new way of living and responding to chaotic situations, one of which is reconciliation.

Reconciliation is simply breaking down the wall that separates us by bringing an end to every irreconcilable matter. Reconciliation is one of the proofs of commitment in a marriage that helps to end fighting and bitterness. We are human and will make mistakes from time to time. But those mistakes must be corrected immediately, because any mistake that is not corrected will only create distance, and distance in the marriage will weaken the bond, making both spouses vulnerable.

[Living as becomes you] with complete lowliness of mind (humility) and meekness (unselfishness, gentleness, mildness), with patience, bearing with one another and making allowances because you love one another. —Ephesians 4:2 (AMPC)

Some of the differences that threaten marriages the most are temperament differences, cultural differences, status differences, and religious differences.

TEMPERAMENT DIFFERENCES

As temperament therapists, we know the importance of couples understanding the uniqueness of and differences in their temperaments, knowing their temperament needs, and how to have a balance in all areas. While one spouse may like to socialize, the other may be uncomfortable around people. One spouse may like to serve, and the other may like to be served. One spouse likes to be in control; the other spouse doesn't like to be controlled. One spouse likes to be hugged and kissed; the other spouse doesn't.

What many consider irreconcilable differences are actually temperament differences. It is therefore paramount that you fully understand your inborn temperaments so you can better understand yourselves. Discovering and understanding each other's God-given temperament will change your marriage for the better. Not only will you be able to identify your strengths and make them stronger, you will also identify your weaknesses and work on them. We always require couples to take a temperament test before we conduct any premarital or marriage counseling. It is a powerful tool and has helped our marriage and other marriages over the years. We highly recommend it.

CULTURAL DIFFERENCES

In today's world, more and more people are falling in love with and marrying people from different cultures. Some spouses hold on too strongly to their culture, and this often takes a toll on the marriage. It is important for you and your spouse to respect each other's culture as much as you can as long as it does not violate your religious principles. Sometimes people get lost in their culture and lose sight of what is right. There are cultures that treat women as second-class citizens. There are cultures where women are abused physically, emotionally, and sexually by their husbands. There are cultures where a woman's place is limited to the kitchen and the bedroom. Just because it is culturally acceptable doesn't mean it is accepted by God. Separate the meat from the bone and embrace only the good of both cultures. Filter every tradition through the Word of God. Never let a man-made tradition destroy your God-made marriage.

And so you break the law of God in order to protect your man-made tradition. And this is only one example. There are many, many others. —Mark 7:13 (TLB)

> **Never let a man-made tradition destroy your God-made marriage**

STATUS DIFFERENCES

Some differences in your status such as education, employment, professional standing, or financial status may have been there before you got married or may have changed during the course of the marriage and should never affect your relationship. There are several reasons why the status of a spouse may change, one of which is child-rearing. You might have agreed that one of you should stay home to raise your children for a period of time or indefinitely. Both must be in agreement. Remember that both are making the sacrifice, so one spouse must not think his or her role is more significant than the other's. Do not threaten or intimidate your spouse with your success. When one succeeds, both succeed. Marriage adds value to you; therefore, whatever you had prior to getting married should be enjoyed by both of you. Never let your status in life drive a wedge between you. Remember that the two are now one.

RELIGIOUS DIFFERENCES

Religion plays a huge role in a marriage. Shared faith is better and will foster spiritual growth, while mixed faith often creates confusion in a marriage, especially when children are involved. Make sure that your religious difference doesn't tear you apart after marriage. The scripture is very clear on this issue.

*For the rest of you who are in mixed marriages—Christian married to non Christian—we have no explicit command from the Master. So this is what you must do. If you are a man with a wife who is not a believer but who still wants to live with you, hold on to her. If you are a woman with a husband who is not a believer but he wants to live with you, hold on to him. The unbelieving husband shares to an extent in the holiness of his wife, and the unbelieving wife is likewise touched by the holiness of her husband. Otherwise, your children would be left out; as it is, they also are included in the spiritual purposes of God. —*1 Corinthians 7:12-14 (MSG)

Decide to be happy and be committed to building your marriage. Be ready and quick to forgive. Express selfless and endless love. Never use divorce as a threat—remove that word from your vocabulary. Wage war against divorce in your marriage. Remember that your words have lasting effects, so use your God-given power of words to change your marriage.

It is not easy to be united with a spouse who does not have the same priorities in life as you do. You both have priorities but may not place them in the same order. They may sometimes overlap, and at other times they may conflict. it is therefore imperative to put things in order. Bridging the differences will make you stronger together. Learn to meet in the middle and agree. Never let your differences tear you apart.

Life is about series of events and every marriage will go through times of storms. Jesus and the disciples experienced a storm while going in the right direction. Jonah was going the wrong direction and also experienced a storm. You may not be able to avoid the storms of life, but you can determine who will be with you during the storm. Keep God with you during your storms, and your marriage will still be standing long after the storms are over. There are different kinds of storms, and they will arise for different reasons: lack of finance, sickness, unemployment, transition, teenage rebellion, blended family, in-laws, and so on. Just make sure you follow these guidelines, and you will come on top of every circumstance.

Exercise: Take turns to ask each other questions #1 and #2 and do #3 together

1. How has being married to me made you a better person?

2. In what ways are we similar? In what ways are we different?

3. Write down your priorities and agree together on their order.

CHAPTER TWELVE

Our God-Made Roles

As society is evolving, so also are the roles of spouses. The roles are no longer as clearly defined as they were previously, when the husband went to work and the wife stayed home to take care of the family. That era is over.

In today's society, women work as much as men work. It is therefore important to know that there is no one perspective on roles, and it is absolutely essential to have flexible role assignments. If you both work, it should not be the sole responsibility of the wife to cook, clean, and take care of the children. Responsibilities and role divisions should be shared depending on your schedules. Failing to deal with rigid role definitions will only create problems, so you must both work together and agree on what is best for your family. Husbands' and wives' roles differs from home to home. Some women are in the workforce, while some men are either stay-at-home fathers or work from home. It is really about what you both agree is best for the family.

Nevertheless, some specific roles in a God-made marriage should never be reversed. We have established that you are two different people and have different responsibilities. A husband taking care of his children and doing household chores is not a reversal of roles, but a wife being the authority in the house is a reversal of role. Understand that marriage relationship provides access. Do not deny your spouse access to the resources God has placed within you or within your reach. Jesus wants us to have what heaven has in store for us. Jesus said, "Whatsoever you ask the Father in my name," "Ask that your joy might be full," "Thy will be done on earth as it is in heaven." This scripture points to relationship with the Father through Jesus providing access to the Father. What's true about this relationship with the Father is also true about your relationship with your spouse. You both have access to each other, so make sure to use those resources well.

A good way to better understand what your spouse is going through and build empathy for each other is to trade places from time to time. Then talk about how you felt, what you learned about your spouse, and how you appreciate each other's unique roles.

Develop the necessary skills needed for role flexibility such as learning how to cook, clean, or change diapers. Have the motivation to change.

Just as we are different in the way we look, we also have our unique roles and functions. The power of your marriage comes from your taking time to be developed and to help each other grow into your unique roles.

GOD-MADE HUSBAND

The word "husband" is derived from "husbandman," which means to care and cultivate. A God-made husband's responsibility is to care and cultivate. Your wife is like a seed and must be protected from every element in the environment that could hinder her growth. You do not damage your seed nor expose her to danger. Protect your seed so she can become fruitful and fulfilled. Seed must produce fruit, and fruit is a visible expression of an inward power. Deal with her like a seed. Nurture her. The words you speak to her should build her up, not tear her down. Your words should make her, not break her.

If you take the time to care and cultivate her, she will blossom. She should be better each year, not worse. Do not ask your wife to do something that you would not do. Your wife is not an accessory; she is an essential. God made you the head, and you should take your God-given responsibilities seriously.

Just as the head helps the body to function to its fullest potential, so also does the husband help his family. Headship is a source of love and nourishment, not pain. Headship at home is not telling your family members what to do, it is showing them what to do. It is simply leading by example. Everything you do should nourish your wife and home. You are the leader, and your leadership as a husband is of serving, not of controlling. You are the foundation and you carry the authority, including spiritual authority, in the home. Therefore, you must not replace your "presence" with "presents."

You are responsible for creating the atmosphere you desire in your home. If you want peace, create an atmosphere of peace. If you want love, create an atmosphere of love. If you want respect, create an atmosphere of respect. You are required by God to perform your active duties in the marriage, with your wife helping as needed. Here are seven key areas of responsibilities of a husband.

PROVIDER

The primary responsibility of a husband is to provide strength and support for his family. He ensures that the needs of his wife and family are met, whether they are spiritual needs, physical needs, emotional needs, or financial needs. He also provides leadership, guidance, safety, and comfort. It is okay if your family dynamic is better with your wife going to work while you take care of the home. Perhaps she makes more money, or your children are young and require one of you to be home with them. But it is not right to leave your family to fend for themselves because you are working. This, of course, must be agreed upon beforehand.

If anyone fails to provide for his own, and especially for those of his own family, he has denied the faith [by disregarding its precepts] and is worse than an unbeliever [who fulfills his obligation in these matters]. —1 Timothy 5:8 (AMP)

LEADER

Part of leadership is choosing not to exert authority when you could. This is particularly important for husbands who think submission is one-sided, from their wives to them alone. The husband's God-given role as the authority over the family does not mean he has to have the final say in every matter. Nor does it give him the right to flex his leadership muscles in every situation. It is not "I wear the pants and I bring home the bacon." It is not "You're wrong and I am right." It is not "I win, you lose." If you win, I win, too. If you lose, I lose. Why? The two have become one. Understand that leadership is responsibility and should therefore be used wisely. Something is wrong If a husband feels the need to constantly tell his wife that he is the head. Perhaps he does not yet understand the scope and depth of his leadership.

Leading is not dominating and being unwilling to change. This also does not mean that the husband gets the blame for every wrong thing that happens in the family.

PROTECTOR

The husband as the primary protector of the marriage provides a safe environment and spiritual guidance for his family. Although the growth is left to individuals in his family as well as the choices they make, he must provide guidance every step of the way. He may not pray as much as the wife does, but this should not stop the wife from praying, studying, or pursuing her personal relationship with God. He should provide physical protection, financial protection, and emotional protection for the family. A husband must not do anything that will put the family in any kind of danger spiritually, physically, financially, or emotionally. The husband must therefore never be the one to inflict pain, hurt, or discomfort to his family. He must make decisions wisely.

DEFENDER

You are not just the protector of your family, you are also a defender. Not only do you protect your wife and children from danger, you must also defend them when they are being criticized by others, especially relatives. Your wife in particular must trust that you will defend her no matter what, and she must be confident that you will always have her back.

PROBLEM SOLVER

Part of the responsibility of the husband is problem solving. He is expected to fix any problems that may arise. A good problem solver knows he will not always have all the answers, so he will consult with his wife, and they both have God to seek for answers.

Lara

Henry used to tell me in the early years of our marriage, "I do not know," or "I do not have an answer for you." That did not sit well with me, and my mouth would go on and on. One day he told me how bad I made him feel that he did not have answers for me. I was smashing him with my words. I repented and began to call him Superman to show my love and support. I bought him a Superman T-shirt, and I saved his number as "Superman" on my cell phone with the "Superman" theme song on purpose. Superman always manages to save the day. I would tell him, "Yes, you can. God will help you." No longer does he say, "I don't know." Now he says, "I don't know yet," then he Googles the answer. He must be the number one fan of Google.

Once I mentioned my hair was breaking and wished I knew a home remedy to use. While I was asleep, he got up to find a solution. I woke up in the morning and he said, "Honey, I found a solution for your hair. It's fresh rosemary and olive oil." I'm like, what? He said, "I Googled it and that was the best of all the home remedies." I was so amazed and touched by it. That's my superman.

PEACEMAKER/PEACE-KEEPER

The husband creates and maintains a peaceful environment for his wife and family. He ensures that nothing disrupts the peace in the home. He ensures everyone in the family is in one accord. He ensures everyone in the family is speaking the same language. Nothing is impossible to accomplish when there is oneness in the marriage, and both spouses are on the same page.

When the Tower of Babel was being constructed, the people began speaking different languages and the project had to be aborted. But when the disciples gathered in the upper room and were in one accord, they understood one another in their own language, and their mission could be accomplished.

The husband ensures that the family Follow One Course Until Successful (F.O.C.U.S.). It is so easy to get caught up in the less important things in life and lose focus on what matters most. The husband therefore sees to it that everyone stays focused on what matters most.

ENCOURAGER

The husband supports and encourages his wife and family. He is their number one fan. He encourages them at every stage of life. His is the voice that says, "I believe in you" and "Yes, you can," when everyone else says, "No way." He is quick to pick them up when they are feeling down. He responds with kindness and assurance regardless of the situation, and this helps his wife and children develop a healthy self-esteem.

What your wife need mostly from you is a listening ear and a caring heart. She should be the most important person in your life after God. Your wife needs your love and affirmation. She may not look or feel beautiful like she used to, but hearing you say she is is important. She is your queen and should be treated as such. Value her opinions and validate what she says, even if you do not agree with her. Allow her to freely express herself. Always remember that she is your helpmeet; she was not created to do everything. Therefore, do not leave everything for her to do.

GOD-MADE WIFE

Scripture tells us that the wife has to help, encourage, and respect her husband. God said, "it is not good for man to be alone; I will therefore make him a helpmeet." This does not in any way imply the wife is her husband's slave or is inferior to him. It means she works alongside him. She is his opposite, and yet they are designed to fit together like a nut and a bolt. She is a partner who always has his best interests at heart. You are an intricate part of your husband. He needs your help, love, and support. You do not complete him; rather, you complement him. Help him fulfill his God-given purpose on earth as he should yours.

Lara

One of my favorite verses in the Bible is Proverbs 18:22 (CEV):

A man's greatest treasure is his wife—she is a gift from the LORD.

Another translation says, *"He who finds a wife finds a good thing and obtains favor from the LORD"* (ESV). I am a good thing! I am Henry's greatest treasure!! Hallelujah!!!

So also, are you the greatest treasure in your husband's life. When he found you, he obtained favor from God. Why? Because the skills, the tools and resources he will need is knitted in you by God. So much that he should never desire anything else from another woman. No one can love and treat him good like you do. No woman can encourage him like you do. No woman can comfort him like you do, and no woman can satisfy him like you do. Your husband needs your affirmation. He may not look or feel like Superman, but your words will make him one. Everything he will ever need in a woman, God has already placed in you. You are his every-woman; it's all in you. So help him in every way you can. Help, do not take over. Look out for his good. Help him be a better man. Help him reduce debt, not incur more debt. Help him better his self-esteem, not shatter it. Help him with your words, don't hurt him. Do not talk down to him; he gets that all day at work. Speak positively into his life on purpose, do not be negative. When he does not believe in himself, you believe in him. When he says, "No, I can't," you say, "Yes, I believe you can."

Look out for each other's best interest because your success is your spouse's success and your spouse failures are your failures. You are one. Whether or not spouses admit it, they need help, especially in areas they are not strong. A wife's job is to help her husband do everything well, not replace him in the home. So when a husband says, "I don't need your help," what he may not realize he is saying is, "I don't need a wife," because it is the job of a wife to help. A husband's refusal of his wife's help will hinder his growth and success. It will hinder him from getting better in life, because her job is to help him become better.

Lara

I am finally at peace with the truth that I am not the head in this marriage, nor am I the neck. I am a helpmeet, a helper. It is so much easier being the helper than being the head. Funny how you pick up some ungodly sayings and run with them. In the early years of our marriage I would often tell my husband, "You might be the head of this marriage, but I am the neck, and the neck controls the head." This was a popular saying even in the church at one point, so I ran with it for a long time until the Word of God made me change to repudiate that saying.

RESPECT

The greatest honor you can give your husband is to respect him.

Lara

When we wrote down our concerns on our first anniversary, I wrote down two pages' worth of

complaints, but Henry wrote down only thing—
"respect."

When the wife speaks, her language must convey respect.
This does not mean that she agrees with everything, but
she can respectfully disagree.

Exercise: Take turns to ask each other questions #1
and #2, and do #3 together.

1. What adjustments do I need to make to better carry
    out my God-made roles?

2. What do you need the most? How can I best provide
    the help and support you need?

3. Talk about each other's strengths and appreciate your
    unique roles.

CHAPTER THIRTEEN

God-Made Marriage Prayers

We truly believe that a couple who prays together stays together. Prayer will strengthen your marriage. Whoever you trust the most will be your first point of contact when your marriage faces tough times. Trust God with your marriage and always go to Him first. If God is your reference point, you will trust Him even when things don't make sense. Trust that God knows what He is doing. Life will throw you a curved ball from time to time, but if you learn to talk to God in prayer, then expect that all things will work out for your good. We trust God with our marriage. We therefore go to Him first in every situation. Do not lean on your own understanding but on God's understanding. Learn to acknowledge God in all of your ways, and He will direct your path.

WORDS OF AFFIRMATION TO EACH OTHER

Words are powerful and should be treated as such. The words you speak to your spouse are very important. Your words can build your spouse up or break them down, so choose your words carefully. At least once a day, intentionally speak words of affirmation to build each other up.

DECLARATION OF LOVE

Declare this together:

Our marriage is God-made; therefore, it will thrive. Our foundation will never be shaken. You are very important to me, and I will never give up on us. I am totally devoted to you and committed to making our marriage better. No matter what comes our way, we will always work it out. I will always give you the attention you need, a listening ear, and a shoulder to cry on. I will wipe away your tears and comfort you. I will be understanding and supportive of you. I will help you and calm your fears. I will always hold you up so you don't fall, fail, break down, or give up. As long as I have breath, I promise to be there for you. I will cherish you for the rest of my days. I will love you daily on purpose, handle you with care forever, and see the best in you always. You're my forever love, my God-made lover.

Take it to the next level by doing the following:

- Do a Seven-Day Words of Affirmation. Complete this sentence daily: "I love you because…"

- Tell each other three areas of strength.

- Reminisce on when you fell in love with each other.

Lara

We take time to pray for each other and our marriage daily. One of my favorite prayers for my marriage is in Romans 8:35, 37–39 (AMP):

> *Who shall ever separate us from the love of Christ? Will tribulation, or distress, or persecution, or famine, or nakedness, or danger, or sword? Yet in all these things we are more than conquerors and gain an overwhelming victory through Him who loved us [so much that He died for us]. For I am convinced [and continue to be convinced—beyond any doubt] that neither death, nor life, nor angels, nor principalities, nor things present and threatening, nor things to come, nor powers, nor height, nor depth, nor any other created thing, will be able to separate us from the [unlimited] love of God, which is in Christ Jesus our Lord.*

> *Be prepared. You're up against far more than you can handle on your own. Take all the help you can get, every weapon God has issued, so that when it's all over but the shouting you'll still be on your feet. Truth, righteousness, peace, faith, and salvation are more than words. Learn how to apply them. You'll need them throughout your life. God's Word is an indispensable weapon. In the same way, prayer is essential in this ongoing warfare. Pray hard and long. Pray for your brothers and sisters. Keep your eyes open. Keep each other's spirits up so that no one falls behind or drops out.* —
Ephesians 6:16–18 (MSG)

HUSBAND'S PRAYER FOR HIS WIFE

Father, I thank you that I found a good wife and obtained favor from You. Thank you that (wife's name) is a blessing to me and a gift from you. Thank you that she is my helpmeet filled with love and care. Help me to see the good in her that I may have overlooked. Help me to see and meet her needs. Help me to love her more each day and to express my love for her. Help me to dwell with her with understanding and always bring out the best in her. This I pray in Jesus' name. Amen.

WIFE'S PRAYER FOR HER HUSBAND

Father, I thank you for my husband, a mighty man of valor. Give him the wisdom he needs as the head of our home and help him to lead our family in the right direction. I know uneasy lies the head that wears the crown, therefore help me to be a supportive wife. Teach me to bring out the best in him always, in Jesus' name. Amen.

COUPLE'S PRAYER FOR THEIR MARRIAGE

Heavenly Father, we thank you for our God-made Marriage. Touch our hearts and draw us closer each day. Bless us and keep us together in love. Help us to be patient with each other. May we live our lives daily on purpose and stay in love with each other. May we always speak the truth in love and value each other. Teach us to respect and honor each other in all that we do. We know there will be seasons of ups and downs. During the difficult times help us never to give up on each other but to know that things will be better. Help us to be understanding and quick to forgive each other. Teach us to walk in unity and integrity. Help us to understand our purpose and fulfill them. May we always demonstrate love, joy, peace, patience, temperance, meekness, and self-control in every situation.

May nothing or no one tear us apart. Help us to remember that we are a team and to always work together as a team. Keep us together and strengthen our bond. May we always be kindhearted and show mercy. Help us to submit to Your will and to each other. We pray for your supernatural protection. Thank you for being the God who supplies all our family's needs; spiritually, emotionally, and financially. Be the center of our marriage and home. Keep our family from danger and hurt. May your Word be the first priority and the final authority in our marriage, in Jesus' name. Amen.

PRAYER FOR WHEN PROBLEMS ARISE

Father, we acknowledge You in this matter. We disallow anything or anyone that will try to disrupt our peace. Let your peace act as umpire in this situation. Give us wisdom to handle this matter properly. Help us to be understanding of each other's feelings and quick in forgiving each other's wrong. Forgive us for any damage our words and actions may have caused. Heal our hearts and help us not to sabotage our marriage by holding on to past hurts, offenses, bitterness, or resentments. Soften our heart toward each other and bring us closer together. Let your unconditional love overflow our hearts, in Jesus' name.

PRAYER FOR THE CHILDREN

Father, thank You for blessing us with our children. Help them to be understanding, forgiving and kindly affectionate to one another. Give us wisdom to guide them in the right path. Surround them with people who will have their best interest at heart. Help them to be focused in their studies and to choose their friends wisely. We declare our children will fulfill their God given destiny and their path will shine brighter each day, in Jesus name.

About the Authors

Henry and Lara Emmanuel are licensed pastors and Clinical Christian Counselors. Their annual God-made marriage retreat has been empowering married couples and has healed several broken marriages. They are also the co-pastors of Christ Abundant Life Ministries, with the vision of saving the lost, changing live and maturing the Saints. Their sons, Tosan and Viomo, are an intricate part of the ministry, and together they are impacting lives in their community and beyond.

CONNECT WITH US ON

 @God-made Marriage & @Godmademarriage

 @Godmademarriage @God_madelove

 @God-Made Marriage

Download the God-Made Marriage Love songs by Lara Emmanuel

God-Made Love and Se Mi Je Je on all digital platforms

For more information on God-made marriage resources, retreat and workshops or to book

Drs. Henry & Lara Emmanuel

www.godmademarriage.com
PHONE:844-4-GOD-MADE
Email: godmademarriage@gmail.com

Address: God-made Marriage
121 Grandview Avenue
Staten Island, New York 10303